HAUNTED NORTH ALABAMA

HAUNTED NORTH ALABAMA

JESSICA PENOT

HAunted
America

Published by Haunted America
A Division of The History Press
Charleston, SC 29403
www.historypress.net

Images are courtesy of the author unless otherwise noted.

First published 2010
Second printing 2012

ISBN 978.1.5402.0482.0

Library of Congress Cataloging-in-Publication Data

Penot, Jessica.
Haunted North Alabama : the phantoms of the South / Jessica Penot.
p. cm.
ISBN 978-1-59629-990-0
1. Ghosts--Alabama. 2. Haunted places--Alabama. I. Title.
BF1472.U6P39 2010
133.109761--dc22
2010027410

Millions of spiritual creatures walk the Earth.
Unseen, both when we wake and when we sleep.

—*John Milton*

CONTENTS

CONTENTS

ACKNOWLEDGEMENTS

.Ihad a lot of help in putting this book together. I would like to thank everyone who helped me in the process. I would especially like to thank all of those who spoke with me and told me their stories. Many of those who contributed to this book did so in confidence, and I am so grateful to have their trust. I would also like to thank those who shared their personal encounters with the supernatural with me. No matter how brief they were, they added to the flavor of the book.

I would especially like to thank the Rison-Dallas Association for sharing its stories and pictures with me. Its stories are a credit to Alabama history and can be found on the association's website: www.rison-dallas.com. I would like to thank every member of the North Alabama Paranormal Meetup who talked with me or let me listen to their stories. They are a great group of people. Leilani, from the Alabama Paranormal Association, was an amazing and invaluable help in making this book possible, and my initial interview with her led me to many of the amazing haunted locations found within this book. I would also like to thank Blair Jett of the Paranormal Research Alliance for all the information he gave me on Crybaby Hollow.

Also, thanks to Jacquelyn Procter Reeves from Huntsville Ghost Walk for all her help and advice. Thanks to every staff member at the haunted locations I visited who gave me the many "off-the-record" stories that made this book much more interesting. I would also like to thank my wonderful husband, Alex Penot, who went with me to explore many haunted sites, supported me through all my research and dealt with my being buried in books and papers for weeks at a time. Thanks to my wonderful sons, who were my partners in crime and traveled with me to almost every haunted location in this book. Finally, thanks to Will McKay, my editor, who found my little blog and helped me turn it into a book

INTRODUCTION

North Alabama is a beautiful and wild place tucked neatly into the rolling hills of the southern Appalachian Mountains. It spreads west into soft plains and rivers. Driving through North Alabama, there are places where you can come to believe you are the last person on earth. The trees are thick, and the undergrowth is thicker. There are many places that still haven't been developed, and there are other places where the development is so thin you can imagine yourself back in the Old South. North Alabama is known for its hiking trails, its beautiful forests and its lakes and rivers. It is an outdoorsman's dream.

It is also known for its ghosts.

Trying to capture the many ghosts of North Alabama is like trying to take a single photograph that tells the story of the history of the region. Ghost stories are history and mythology delicately intertwined. By exploring the ghost stories of North Alabama, I discovered not only its past but also its present. I learned about the spirit of the region.

Most of the ghost stories contained here start in the past. They start with a tragedy and then are spread through oral tradition and folklore. Finding this folklore is harder than finding a book on history; one must travel and talk to the people who keep these histories and get them to share their stories. Of course, many don't want their names known, and many don't want to talk at all. In order to respect the privacy of the multitude of people I spoke with, I left many names out of this book.

North Alabama's history is complicated. Alabama's story began in antiquity with the natives of the land. These peoples lived in the North Alabama region for over ten thousand years. The final native inhabitants of North Alabama were the Cherokee tribe. The Cherokee people were eventually overwhelmed by a steady influx of European settlers. Many of these Europeans brought slaves with them. In his book on southern economics, Randall Miller describes these Europeans as having a culture that was rooted in the countryside. He says that their values were anti-progress, as well as honor, gentility and a highly ordered social scale. Alabama history prior to the Civil War is rooted in these values; it was the Deep South and the Old South.

Many of the ghosts found in North Alabama folklore and history are from the years that the Civil War set the South on fire. A few are from the years prior to that, when southern gentility and culture ruled. White lady ghost stories lend themselves to tragic southern belles.

White ladies are one of the many archetypes that can be found in ghost stories throughout the world. They are tragic women. They have often died violent deaths and are usually of the upper class. They are almost always described as beautiful. There are several other archetypes you might find in this collection of ghost stories. The crying child is a common theme in ghost stories and is usually associated with the death of a young child or baby. The chained man is one of the earliest archetypes and was first seen in the Middle Ages in Europe. Soldier ghosts are some of the most prevalent in the world, and this book is filled with this kind of ghost. Soldier ghosts can be found on battlefields and in forts, but they can also be found in the soldier's home, where he may linger long after his death.

Alabama history is perfect for many of these types of ghost stories. The years that followed the Civil War were filled with enough sadness and hardship to generate a book of ghost stories. Following the Civil War, North Alabama had to redefine itself economically. It had prospered when cotton was in high demand in the 1820s and 1830s, but by the Civil War, the soil was exhausted and the cotton market was flooded. North Alabama was economically crippled by the Civil War, and the plantation and agrarian economy on which it was built was no longer sustainable. During the antebellum period, North Alabama embraced change and invited manufacturers from the North to help it rebuild its broken economy. Mills flooded into Alabama and dominated the North Alabama culture and economy for many years to follow.

North Alabama was also able to use its abundant natural resources to rebuild its economy. It quarried out limestone, iron, ore and coal. Birmingham, Alabama, was able to turn itself into a steel center by the turn of the century, and many quarries opened throughout North Alabama. The area's history began to change into a history of regional culture and economics as different areas banked on their own resources and strengths.

Huntsville, Alabama, was able to define itself by the work of one man. It stood on his shoulders and built itself up as one of the top aerospace industrial cities in the nation. It stepped away from the rest of North Alabama and began importing its labor pool from all over the world. It now has a community and culture that is more global than southern. Smaller towns continued with their agrarian and small-town manufacturing roots. That culture remained much the same. Many towns built their economies on the growing educational demands of the region and turned their old college campuses into thriving universities where education flourishes. Towns like Florence, Alabama, were able to turn very old schools into modern learning centers. Birmingham, Alabama, on the southernmost tip of North Alabama, broke free from its steel and fire past. The construction of the University of Alabama in Birmingham would help it define itself as the biomedical capital of Alabama, where state-of-the-art medical technology and research have become defining features of the city.

North Alabama as it is today is culturally diverse, and each city and rural community defines itself by its own history. Florence, Alabama, is very different from Huntsville, Alabama, and Huntsville is very different from Cullman. North Alabama was once unified by one set of values and beliefs, but those days have faded. In writing this book, I tried to capture a piece of the diversity that is North Alabama. I tried to explore the different parts of its history and culture and create one portrait of an amazingly diverse region. The ghosts within this book tell the story of the region's history. They also tell their own tales of horror and sorrow. They fill dark corners with fear and give you reasons to be afraid of the dark.

DEAD CHILDREN'S PLAYGROUND

Maple Hill Playground is a place that has become legend. In Huntsville, Alabama, this playground has become a rite of passage for local youths, who are challenged to hop over the gates at night and creep into the shadows of the tall trees through complete darkness. The playground is pressed up against Maple Hill Cemetery, so as they walk down the road to the playground, they can see the tombstones illuminated by the moonlight. It is a short walk up the road from the fence to the playground. The playground is set off the road, and the earth curves downward into a rocky cove. It is surrounded on all sides by sheer rock cliffs that have been overgrown with kudzu and greenery.

The youths who come here sit on the swings and wait for the legends to come to life. They wait for the dead children to come out of the shadows of night and play. They must be brave, because they all know the stories. There are literally hundreds of them. They've all heard about people who have vanished into the shadows of this playground and of teenagers who have never been seen again. These legends are so strong in Huntsville that the true name of this playground has been forgotten. No one knows the name Maple Hill Playground; everyone calls it Dead Children's Playground, where the ghosts of lost children spend their nights endlessly playing in the dark.

Dead Children's Playground.

The legends surrounding this playground are prolific. One local legend says that in the early 1960s, Huntsville, Alabama, was the prowling grounds of a child murderer. This murderer abducted local children and did horrible things to them before killing them. When he was done with them, he buried them in the walls of the playground. The playground is filled with the bodies of these lost children, and when darkness settles and the gates of the playground are closed, they rise up and make the playground their own. Of course, according to Huntsville Parks and Recreation, Maple Hill Playground wasn't built until 1985, long after these murders were supposed to have taken place, but facts don't stop the legend from spreading and growing.

Most of the legends surrounding this playground also say that it is part of beautiful Maple Hill Cemetery. Maple Hill Cemetery is the largest cemetery in Alabama and one of the oldest. Founded in 1818, Maple Hill now covers over one hundred acres of land. It has its own encyclopedia of ghost stories associated with it that seems to seep out of the tombstones into the neighboring playground. Those who believe the legends associated with

The view from the parking lot.

Dead Children's Playground say that it was built for the children of the dead, to bring solace to those who had suffered loss. It is interesting that the oldest marker in Maple Hill Cemetery actually belongs to a child. The oldest grave with its marker intact is that of Mary Frances Atwood, infant daughter of William and Martha Caroline Atwood, who died September 17, 1820. This gravestone might mark the beginning of what was to become a strong connection between the cemetery and the ghosts of children.

Legends aside, the real history of the playground is much less interesting. The playground was a rock quarry bought and mined from 1945 to 1955. During this time, Alabama was known for its limestone and marble quarries, and several such quarries were mined in the region. The playground's history as a quarry accounts for its covelike appearance and the high cliff faces that surround the playground. The playground is actually built into the side of a gentle hill that was mined out and used for limestone. The cliffs are not natural. After the quarry closed in 1955, the land was donated to the city. In 1985, the city turned this bundle of land into Maple Hill Park.

Maple Hill Park is more than just the playground. If you drive farther down the road, you'll find another covelike area with grassy space that can be used for sports. Although there are no current sporting events at the park, it is clearly designed for soccer and other outdoor activities. The park also includes a pavilion for picnics and gatherings. It could even be used for a birthday party. Maple Hill Park is not part of the cemetery and never was. It is part of the City of Huntsville's Parks and Recreation Department and Youth Athletic Zone 3. The playground was remodeled in 2002 and now sports modern playground equipment and a new picnic pavilion. The park is 8.64 acres—a sizeable and beautiful spot for a family to spend the day. If you didn't know about the cemetery or the legends, this would be an almost perfect park.

The park is quite beautiful, and the covelike surroundings give it a feeling of seclusion, despite its urban setting. The park is also uncommonly quiet, and even during the day, it feels off the beaten path. Tall trees create permanent shadows, and from the playground, which is set in a recess where the old quarry must have been, you can't see the road or any other activity. You can almost imagine that you are deep in the woods, far away from the rest of the world.

The day I ventured out to the playground, I spent quite a bit of time filming and watching. It was sunny, but it had just rained, so there were enormous puddles under the swings prohibiting the living from swinging. Despite this, the swings moved gently back and forth. Birds sang in the background, and the sun filtered in through the tree branches, painting the earth in dappled light. There was no wind, yet the movement perpetuated, and I was able to capture five minutes of the swings gently moving on their own. There may be some natural explanation for this phenomenon that escapes me. I'm not the only one who has recorded this trend. YouTube is filled with videos of these swings moving, and many visitors to the park describe this trend.

The swings aren't the only ghostly activity that observers describe. One visitor I spoke with described hearing children laughing. Another person I talked to said that she had heard a child crying while she was visiting the playground. One visitor claims to have seen even more significant paranormal activity; he claims to have witnessed a ghost child leaping from the moving swing and then coming to a complete stop. Another witness claims to have heard the voices of a child and a woman calling to each

The swings that always seem to move.

other. Stories like this are as numerous as the stars in the sky. Everyone who travels to the playground comes back with another story. Ribbons of light and ghostly shadows are seen in photos that visitors have brought back from the park.

My photos aren't that interesting, nor did I witness any of this activity during my stay at the park. I have visited during the day and during the night, and all I heard was bird song or the chirp of crickets and the constant groaning of the moving swings.

The Alabama Paranormal Society (APS) did a study of Dead Children's Playground. I was fortunate enough to talk to Leilani of APS. She told me that the playground was very active and very haunted. Leilani has been ghost hunting for years, and she is also a psychic. While she was at the playground, she saw the ghost of a woman in Victorian garb. It was the most apparent and clear ghost she was able to see, but she felt others. APS's investigation indicated that the ghosts that come to playground come from the cemetery. They are wanderers. They are not directly connected to the playground itself. They merely drift in and out of the wooded park that is pressed up against the necropolis. Their story is the story of those who lie in the graveyard.

Although I am not a psychic, there is definitely something eerie about this little playground. It is too calm and too serene, and the view of the cemetery makes this calmness unnerving. Living children rarely play in this picture-perfect park, so it is left mostly to the dead.

THE HAUNTING OF THE UNIVERSITY OF NORTH ALABAMA

In order to get to the University of North Alabama (UNA), you have to drive the back roads of rural Alabama. You have to drive past schools and old cemeteries. You have to go through many small towns and pieces of Alabama that a city dweller might never see. On your way, you'll pass a closed Halloween haunted house and a year-round Christmas castle. You'll pass flea markets and historic polo clubs, and at the end of this journey, you'll come to one of the most beautiful university campuses in Alabama. It is so beautiful that it seems out of place. It seems like it should be part of an Ivy League school or a piece of an old English manor. This is the University of North Alabama. It is not only one of the most beautiful campuses in Alabama, but it is also the most haunted.

As you wander through the old campus, history will come to life around you. The old buildings surround the cobblestoned pedestrian campus. Their blackened windows loom above the green grass and fragrant flowers. The center of campus is marked by a large marble fountain that sputters out crystal-clear water. To the right of the fountain is a lion habitat with a waterfall and two lions. Small children stand around the habitat with their faces pressed up against the glass, gazing in wonder at the two majestic beasts. The buildings around the quad are all Gothic Revival style, making the campus seem even older than it actually is.

The University of North Alabama.

The university is old. It was founded in 1855 after the president of LaGrange University fled across the Tennessee River. The president founded Wesleyan University after LaGrange University was burned to the ground by Union forces. Like many places in the South, Wesleyan University was forged in the furnace of the Civil War. Both Union and Confederate troops occupied the buildings of Wesleyan at points during the war. After the war, in 1872, the Methodist Church gave Wesleyan University to the State of Alabama, and it was renamed the State Northern School of Florence. It was the first coeducational college in the United States. The school changed names many times in the following years and was finally named the University of North Alabama in 1974.

The school has grown since that time, and the campus has been shaped into the beautiful university it is today. UNA is now home to about seventy-one hundred students. It has sixty undergraduate majors and many postgraduate degrees. The campus occupies 130 acres in the heart of Florence, Alabama.

The oldest building on the UNA campus is Wesleyan Hall. This three-story building is also the most striking building on campus. From far away, it

Wesleyan Hall.

looks almost like a castle. Its Gothic-style turrets and architecture are part of the most impressive building in Florence. Today, Wesleyan Hall is home to the Geography, Psychology and Foreign Language Departments. Its halls are crowded with students rushing to class or studying at the desks against the walls. Its walls are filled with large colorful posters documenting the many research projects and publications completed by the faculty and students of the hall's many departments.

Wesleyan Hall was designed by Adolphys Heiman, although some believe that one of Heiman's slaves may have actually designed the building. It was constructed by Zebulon Pike Morrison and served as the university for many years. During the Civil War, Union troops occupied Wesleyan Hall. During General Sherman's notorious march through the South, Wesleyan Hall was one of his stops. Sometime between 1863 and 1864, Sherman came to Wesleyan Hall. It is said that the Florence residents gave Wesleyan Hall to Sherman in exchange for him leaving the rest of the city alone. Sherman would not burn Florence because he was given Wesleyan as his home while he visited.

During the Civil War, it was not uncommon for officers to bring their sons to act as drummer boys. One of Sherman's colonels brought his son with him as a drummer boy. The son was named Jeremiah. No one is entirely sure what happened to Jeremiah. The cause of his demise is more legend than fact. Some say he was abducted by locals and held for ransom. Others claim that he went for a walk and drowned in the creek near Wesleyan Hall. Whatever the cause, his ghost has been seen wandering the corridors of this old building ever since Sherman left.

There have been numerous reports of sightings of Jeremiah's ghost. Some see his waterlogged form standing in the halls, and others hear his footsteps on the floorboards. There are those who describe hearing his voice, and many say they've seen him walking across the lawn in the light of the moon.

Jeremiah is not alone in his ghostly wanderings. There is another young ghost that haunts the University of North Alabama campus. The ghost of a very young girl wanders with him. This little girl, Molly, is one of the most famous haunts of Florence, and she can be found at the off-campus bookstore.

The off-campus bookstore.

Molly's story is quite tragic. Tradition says that the bookstore was once her house. She lived there with her mother and father. They were a happy family, but Molly was lonely. She spent her days playing alone in her room with her dolls. The little girl's father was particularly worried about his baby's loneliness, so he went out and purchased an adorable little puppy for her. Of course, the girl was delighted. It was love at first sight. She loved the puppy so much that she put it in bed with her that night, and the two little ones nestled up next to each other in the soft evening light. She slept like this with her puppy for several nights. The two curled up next to each other in peaceful slumber.

Both of Molly's parents were happy with the new puppy, and they felt as if they had found a good friend for their little girl. It came as a complete surprise when they were awakened one night to the sound of Molly screaming. The wail cut through the night, awakening both parents and sending them running into their daughter's room. The puppy had bit the little girl. The parents were mortified, but the girl and the puppy seemed no worse for the wear, so they wrote off the event as caused by the types of bad dreams that sometimes haunt little dogs. Things returned to normal, but it wasn't long before the dog and the little girl began to show signs of illness. The parents took the little girl to the doctor, and both she and the puppy were diagnosed with rabies. According to legend, the disease had progressed too far for treatment, and both died shortly thereafter.

Time went on, and the building was turned into a fraternity house. The house was remodeled, and the fraternity members reported seeing a phantom girl sitting in the second-story window gazing out. It wasn't just the frat boys who saw her. People walking by the house reported seeing her as well. The building is an off-campus bookstore now, and people still see the little girl looking longingly out the window. The women who work at the bookstore don't deny her presence. They say she still makes her appearances, sometimes alone and sometimes with her dog. One employee I spoke with said that she has never seen or heard Molly, but she claims that every morning some of the candy is missing from the shelf.

The Shoals Ghost Walk visits the bookstore regularly, and many who have taken this tour have reported seeing Molly's ghost. One ghost walker even managed to snap a picture of the little girl standing in the corner. Those who have heard Molly say she always says the same thing. She always asks, "Have you seen my dog?"

Coby Hall.

Coby Hall sits directly across the street from the off-campus bookstore. It is a pretty building. It sits in the shade of several large, lazy oaks. It isn't part of the central campus and differs architecturally from the main campus. Its Classic architecture is typical of the Old South. It is the admissions building for University of North Alabama and is quite welcoming. When you step inside, the staff members greet you cheerfully. They will talk to you about just about anything and are happy to discuss the beautiful building they are overjoyed to work in.

Coby Hall, one of the most recent additions to UNA's campus, was donated to the university in 1990 by David Brubaker in memory of his wife, Coby Stockard Brubaker. It was named after her. Coby Hall was built in 1830 by John Simpson. John Simpson moved to Florence to buy land and start a mercantile business. Like many of the Irishmen of the time, he came to chase the American dream. Mr. Simpson found the American dream, and his little business flourished in Florence. He became a very wealthy man. He was envied by all, not just for his wealth and success, but also for his beautiful wife, Margaret Patton. Margaret Patton was a notorious beauty in her day, and she was beloved by all who laid eyes on her.

When Mr. Simpson built Coby Hall, he named it Courtland Mansion. It was the perfect home for his beautiful bride. Mrs. Simpson was said to adore her house. She decorated it with great love and spent a considerable amount of time entertaining. Mrs. Simpson was a perfectionist, and every detail of the house was perfect, especially when she had a party. Nothing was ever out of place. Every item of her home was laid out to make each room an exercise in beauty.

I spoke with an employee who works in Coby Hall. She described the ghost that haunts Coby Hall in graphic detail. She says that it is Mrs. Simpson's ghost who wanders the halls of Coby Hall and that Mrs. Simpson still gets mad when something is out of place. Mrs. Simpson is especially irritable when there is a wedding at Coby Hall. She said that Mrs. Simpson can't stand all the disarray in her house, and this leads to an increase in paranormal activity.

Mrs. Simpson.

One woman told me of a Saturday that she spent at work. She had gone down into the basement to gather some things she needed. There was to be a wedding at Coby Hall in a few hours, and she knew she needed to leave quickly. She heard chairs banging around in the basement while she was there. It was quite a commotion. She didn't pay much attention to the commotion because she assumed that the caterers had arrived and had begun preparing for the event.

When she went upstairs, she was quite surprised to find the house empty. There were no vehicles around the house, and no one seemed to be there. Flustered, she looked around for the caterers again but found no one. The caterers arrived a few hours later. She questioned them about the commotion, but they insisted they hadn't been there. They had just arrived. The employee now knows that it was Mrs. Simpson in the basement. Her ghost was angry about the furniture that had been recently moved and was putting it back in place.

THE MOODY BRICK

Shadows cling to the corners of the Moody Brick like paste. Even in daylight, it seems to occupy a dark space that many locals avoid. The house is surrounded by horror stories of mass murders and death. Stories of slave uprisings and slaughters haunt the house's history. Those who have visited the Moody Brick at night come back with stories of phantom women and ghostly lights.

The Moody Brick is a two-story house in Kyles, Alabama. It is an L-shaped structure made of red brick. The architectural styles in the house aren't consistent. There is a lack of symmetry that shows that the house has crumbled and been rebuilt in different styles at many different times. There is a cemetery across the country road from the house, and two other cemeteries dot the landscape.

Much of the history of the Moody Brick isn't exact. It was built before 1855, although the exact date of its construction is unknown. It was built for Carter Overton Harris and his wife, Mary Ann Hudson. It is believed that the house may have been built by Hiram Higgins, who designed the old courthouses in Scottsboro and Moulton, Alabama. He also designed several school buildings in both Athens and Talladega. Although Higgins's work on the house isn't documented, he left stylistic indicators in the brick structure and the pilasters.

There are many stories about the Moody Brick's history, although most of the stories can't be confirmed. The period of time around and before the Civil War is particularly mucky. It is known that the owners of the Moody Brick kept slaves prior to the Civil War, and evidence of this can be seen in the slave cemetery that is still on the property. The treatment of the slaves by their owners has been the source of a great many rumors. According to local stories, the owners of the old plantation were particularly cruel to their slaves. Locals say that the family may have beaten, chained and even killed slaves in the dank, dark basement beneath the Moody Brick. The legends say that the neighbors never reported this activity to the authorities because some bad treatment of slaves was expected. However, it did make the locals talk and was shocking even to old southerners. The rumors and gossip that spread about the deplorable treatment of the slaves trickled down through time, so even today, many locals know about the evil that happened in the basement of the Moody Brick.

If this local lore is to be believed, after the Civil War the slaves had their revenge. Many believe that just following the war, the slaves rose up and killed many of their owners in their beds. They say that the slaves could take no more abuse, so they slaughtered their masters and fled into the night.

With the help of the Ku Klux Klan, the ex-slaves were rounded up and caught. A lynch mob served them the justice of the Old South, and the ex-slaves were hanged from the tree in front of the Moody Brick. There is no written documentation of these events, but the oral traditions are strong, and many believe them. I learned of this history while I was investigating another haunted location. A friendly resident was more than happy to point me in the direction of the Moody Brick and tell me its many dark stories.

According to tradition, the Moody Brick served as a hospital during the Civil War. This is consistent with historical accounts of the time, as many large plantation houses and farmhouses were used as hospitals. Between 1863 and 1864, the building served as a hospital for the Chattanooga and Chickamauga campaigns. The floors were lined with the injured and dying soldiers of the Confederate army. Eventually, the Yankees took the farm and used it for their own purposes before they burned it to the ground. They left evidence of their visit behind, and that evidence remains. One of the three cemeteries that surround the Moody Brick is a Yankee Civil War cemetery.

The house fell into significant disrepair following the Civil War. It became a burned-out, overgrown husk of a house that time almost left behind. The house changed hands in 1872, when it was bought by the Moodys. In 1877, the *Alabama Herald* described the Moody Farm. The author of the article detailed the disrepair that had taken over, calling the house abused and neglected. He said that the Moody Farm was

> *in a woefully dilapidated condition—the fences all down—the land grown up in sedge grass and bushed—the hill sides all washed off—and the fine brick building so much abused and neglected, as to present an inviting retreat for ghosts and hob-goblins generally.*

He then went on to describe the hard work the Moodys had put into repairing the farm and making it beautiful again. He said that the plantation had been exhausted by the heavy planting of cotton. The soil had to rest, and in the meantime, the Moodys had planted oats and wheat. He also noted the many tenant cottages and the mill that were part of the farm at the time.

In 1888, the Moody Farm was destroyed by fire. A spark from the chimney fell on the roof, and the house burned down. The house was rebuilt, but it wasn't rebuilt in any consistent style. Now the house is Greek Revival on the outside with a Victorian front door. Inside, two mantles are from the Federal period, two are Italianate and two are Victorian. The porch is Italianate. Further additions later on added to this general disconnect in style. In 1901, ornate stenciling and ceiling paintings were added to the house. All of this makes the house feel slightly disjointed in its beauty so that nothing quite goes together in the right way.

The house stayed in the Moody family for some time. The Moody family cemetery on the property bears witness to this. The tombstones show that Ms. Josephine Moody Sanders married Mr. Pleasant Wyatt Sanders. They lost a son, Charley B. Sanders, at the house in 1913, but Pleasant Sanders didn't die until 1935. There are three known cemeteries on the Moody Brick's property. The first is the Moody family cemetery. Within it, there are seven clearly marked graves and one large block wall. No one knows who is buried within the wall. The other cemeteries on the property are a slave cemetery and the Yankee cemetery. Some claim that there are two more cemeteries on the properties with less well-marked or completely unmarked graves.

No one knows for sure which ghosts haunt the Moody Brick. There are so many stories that it is hard to know how many spirits wander the grounds. Some say there have been numerous unexplained deaths there over the years. There is a story about a maid who lived there for a time. It is said that she took her own life by jumping from the balcony. Others say that there were numerous construction accidents there during the times when the Moody Brick was being renovated and repaired. They say that one of the builders fell to his death in an accident and another killed himself. Some locals are afraid to visit the Moody Brick. They believe that those who walk on its darkened grounds are doomed to die a fearful death. They say the place is cursed.

One woman I heard from defended the Moody Brick. She said that she had been there and it was in fabulous condition; she could see no evidence of a haunting. She thought all the ghost talk was nonsense and said that there was no evidence of any deaths on the property. However, there are many who would disagree.

One visitor to the Brick said she went there to take pictures of the house. While she was there, she saw an entire host of ghosts. She got out of the car and took pictures, and while she was shooting the house, she saw a woman in white walk across the yard from the graveyard toward the house. She also saw the ghosts of what she believed to be slaves in chains standing beside the house and men dressed in Civil War uniforms toward the back of the house. This visitor claimed she captured these ghosts in the photographs she took.

Another visitor says that he hasn't been to the Moody Brick since the latest restoration. He visited at night. He claims that he saw a woman in white looking down at him from the window above. It was enough to send him running to his car. This visitor said that he hadn't believed in ghosts before, but after one visit to the Moody Brick, he was a believer.

The woman in white appears to be the most commonly seen ghost at the Moody Brick, and tales of her standing in the window with a candle are as prolific as the rain. It is hard to say who this lonely lady is. She has been seen coming from the cemetery, so she could be the ghost of Josephine, who rests with her young son buried next to her, or she could be the ghost of the maid who took her own life from the very window the ghost is often seen in. There is so much sorrow at the Moody Brick that it is hard to know for sure.

Although it is hard to name the ghosts at the Moody Brick—and there will always be those who say there are no ghosts there at all—the legends of this old building will carry on. They have lived here for over 150 years, and those who visit will continue to tell stories of tragic white ladies, the ghosts of tortured slaves, murdered masters and Civil War phantoms.

THE OLD DALLAS MILL
AND VILLAGE

The Old Dallas Mill site isn't much to look at. It is a patch of grass by the overpasses. It is a bit of earth and dirt filled with litter and grime, hidden beneath I-565. It isn't in the best part of town. Traffic passes overhead, filling the air with constant noise. You wouldn't know that anything interesting or important ever hid in the shadows of the overpasses. If you were just driving by, you wouldn't stop to look or realize that this patch of dirt had once been a thriving mill and village. You wouldn't know that it is haunted by the ghosts of those who died in the ashes of the mill when it burned to the ground.

On more careful study, you might find a plaque. The plaque says that this was once a historic place. It says that a mill stood here, built in 1890 by T.B. Dallas, and the old ruined shell of a building once housed Alabama's largest cotton manufacturer. It explains that the mill was once part of a microcosm and was a city unto itself up until 1949. Mr. Dallas created a small world of his own in the area that is now pavement, dirt and the underbelly of the interstate. He provided housing, churches, schools, libraries, lodge buildings and a YMCA for his employees, and a little village grew and thrived in his generosity. This little village was called the Dallas Village.

In 1891, when the mill's construction was announced in the old *Huntsville Times*, the city of Huntsville greeted this news with widespread excitement.

Water tower at the old mill site. *Courtesy of the Dallas-Rison Association.*

The city of Huntsville had a population of 1,327 citizens at the time, and this was big news for a small town. The *Huntsville Times* did regular updates on the progress of the mill, and one article in the paper celebrated the near completion of the 350-foot-long factory. The journalist marveled at the five-story building that required eighteen hundred operatives to run.

The mill was completed in 1892 and began operation in that same year. When the mill was finished, it was surrounded by the comfortable homes that had also been built by Dallas for the use of his employees. This neighborhood in the shadow of the mill was called the *Dallas Village*. The mill's village was almost as large as the city of Huntsville itself at that time and extended from what is now Oakwood Avenue to Dallas Street. The village grew and prospered over time. In 1921, the mill was able to open its own freestanding school, the Rison School for the children of the millworkers. The little village had fourteen different stores, and the school is still celebrated by its former students today. One former student of the Rison School and resident of Dallas Village reports that those were simpler times. He says that in those days there were no video games and no television, so all the children learned to play poker, not for the gambling but just for fun.

Newspaper articles from 1904 and 1905 describe several small fires that occurred within the small Dallas Village. They describe the fires and their damage but then proudly report that Dallas Village, as the *Old Huntsville Magazine* noted, "has the most remarkable record of any village its size in the county. Until Saturday morning there had never been a fire in the village proper for thirteen years." This claim is made sadly ironic by the fact that both of the ghosts reported to haunt the old mill died in fires.

The little village prospered until 1949, when the Dallas Mill was closed. Times had changed. Since the Civil War, mills had dominated North Alabama's economy, but by the 1940s that dominance was fading. It took six years for the floundering little village that had depended on the mill for its livelihood to give up and allow itself to be incorporated into Huntsville proper. This was the end of an era for the residents of Dallas Village. The Rison School limped along for several more years. In 1967, the high school was demolished, and in the '70s the elementary school was turned into a day care. It, too, was finally demolished to make way for the interstate. The village surrounding the mill fell victim to similar circumstances. Some homes burned down, and others were demolished to make way for Huntsville's growing population.

In 1955, Genesco Shoe Company bought out the Dallas Mill, and Genesco kept the doors to the old mill open until 1985. In 1985, the Genesco Shoe Company closed, the windows were boarded up and the building became vacant.

The stories of the ghosts of the old mill are stories of fire. The first man said to haunt the vacant remains of the mill died while cleaning the smokestacks in the early twentieth century. His ghost has been said to haunt the mill for many years. The second ghost that still wanders this mill site is a homeless man who had taken up residence in the mill after it was vacated. This man had found shelter in the unused building and found some sense of security there. Unfortunately, in 1992, the building caught on fire. The fire burned for three longs days and painted the skies of Huntsville orange with its fury. There was little left of the homeless man. All that remains of him is his ghost.

Legend says that the site of the old mill is still haunted by these ghosts. They wander the area where the mill once stood. Those who drive by have described seeing lonely figures in the dark.

I drove out to the old mill site to study its remains and look for any evidence of the ghosts within. I wandered the area where it once stood looking for any evidence of what had once stood so tall and proud. There was no sign of movement, and the many pictures I took added nothing to the stories of phantom faces in the dark. But the stories persist, and whoever haunts the shadows of the old mill doesn't plan to leave.

THE GHOSTS OF
MERRIMACK HALL

M errimack Hall is tucked neatly away in the west end of Huntsville. The
building itself seems oddly out of place here. It is surrounded by tacky
strip malls and modern buildings that all appear a bit shabby and run-down.
The road in front of it is loud and busy. Everything about this part of West
Huntsville is dingy and colorless. Merrimack Hall steps out of this setting
like a peacock in a barnyard. It is a pretty building that has been lovingly
restored to its former beauty. It is inviting, and before you even walk in, you
begin to wonder what lurks inside.

Inside, the building is just as beautiful as it is outside. The building was
restored by the Jenkinses, who have turned it into a nonprofit performing arts
center and a community resource. The walls inside are covered with playbills
and programs from all the performances that have run at this community
center. They are also covered in newspaper articles and stories about the
way the Merrimack Hall Performing Arts Center has given back to the
community. It is hard to imagine any ghosts in this exciting environment,
but the ghosts at Merrimack Hall are so active and so dark that they have
turned skeptics into believers and made brave men quake.

The Merrimack wasn't always a performing arts center, but it has always
been a community center. In the early part of the twentieth century,
Alabama was ruled by large mills and the microcosms that grew up around

Merrimack Hall.

them. Huntsville, Alabama's history reflects this trend. Large mills sprang up around the area that is now Huntsville, and in the shadow of these mills villages grew and thrived. Mill owners provided their employees with housing, schools and all of their needs.

Merrimack Textile Mill was one of the largest and most successful of the Alabama mills. In July 1900, Merrimack Manufacturing Company of Lowell, Massachusetts, opened its textile mill in Huntsville, and the first village houses appeared in its shadows. When the mill began operations, it had 750 employees who lived in sixty houses clustered around the mill. The Merrimack Mill was an instant success, and demand for the mill's textiles seemed to grow immediately. This large demand led to the construction of a second mill in 1903.

So the Merrimack Village expanded, and more houses were built. In order to serve the growing population of the Merrimack Village, the building that is now Merrimack Hall was constructed. This early structure served many purposes. It was a community center even then and was used to house a small school for children, a bicycle shop, a photo shop and two barbershops.

In 1914, a freestanding school was added to the village, and the plan for Merrimack Hall was changed. In 1920, Merrimack Hall was renovated and rebuilt into a twenty-five-thousand-square-foot community center that would house a gymnasium, two community rooms, a store, a pharmacy, a barbershop, a library and a scout meeting room, an auditorium and a café. Merrimack became a popular hangout for the young people of the village. Merrimack Hall became the location for all of the major social events of the village. There were basketball games in the gymnasium and scout activities in the scout room. One community room was used for men's activities, and dances were held in the gymnasium. There was a youth room for the young people and a baseball diamond behind the hall for baseball games. Merrimack Hall was the center of life for the residents of the village.

Time changes all things, and after World War II, Huntsville underwent many major shifts. Many of the other mills in the area were being shut down, and their mill villages were being incorporated into the Huntsville city limits. The Dallas Mill closed its doors in 1949. It wasn't surprising that the Merrimack Mill was sold to M. Lowenstein in 1946. The Merrimack Textile Company became Huntsville Textiles. Lowenstein purchased the mill and decided to improve and renovate the facility. He increased the workforce by almost three hundred and renovated and modernized the entire facility. Renovations and improvements to Merrimack Hall were part of his improvements. The hall was enlarged, and a teen canteen was added for the young people. Movies were shown at Merrimack Hall on a regular basis.

The mill and the mill village continued to prosper as Huntsville Textiles and became the leading textile manufacturer in the Southeast. The number of employees increased to almost sixteen hundred, and regular renovations and modernizations to both the mills and Merrimack Hall kept the community and the business thriving. Slowly, the village began to merge with the city as Huntsville grew up around it. Mill children began to go to the local schools, and Huntsville utilities became a necessary part of life. By the 1980s, the mill was finally beginning to show signs of decline. It was the last of the Huntsville mills to close, and although it stood the test of time better than the other mills, it still had to surrender to historical inevitability. In 1988, the mill was sold, and in 1992 it was demolished. Merrimack Hall was forgotten until it was rediscovered by the Jenkinses.

Now, Merrimack Hall has been given a new breath of life. It has been turned into a community center again and has rediscovered itself as a place where stage dreams are made real. But the ghosts of those who used to enjoy Merrimack Hall haven't moved on. They still cling to their old community center, and they don't want to let go. Merrimack Hall has been the site of continual paranormal activity since its reopening and renovation. Those who have been to the hall have heard phantom voices and have seen doors close by themselves and objects move on their own. Some say that Merrimack is haunted by a little boy named Charlie Foster, who worked in the mill before child labor laws made this illegal. They say that Charlie wanders the community center—the center of his world in life—making mischief.

The Alabama Paranormal Association (APS) investigated the haunting at Merrimack Hall. The Alabama Paranormal Association is a nonprofit group that investigates paranormal activity using technology and reason. It uses instrumental readings, eyewitness accounts and history to assess and evaluate whether a location is haunted. I spoke with Leilani from APS about the group's findings at Merrimack Hall. According to Leilani, Merrimack Hall is one of the most active haunted sites she has investigated. She believes that multiple spirits haunt the site and that Charlie Foster isn't the only ghost clinging to the old building.

APS reports that it was able to catch several apparitions on film. Leilani also describes hearing voices, singing and footsteps on the stage during the investigation. She says that she had a man who was quite skeptical with her. He said that he absolutely didn't believe in ghosts, but after he saw a full apparition of a man sitting in a chair, he changed his mind. Other evidence that APS caught during its investigation included a very interesting electronic voice phenomena (EVP) recording. During this recording, an investigator asked if the ghosts liked the Christmas lights, and a voice on the tape distinctly answered, "Yes." One of the investigators had brought his iPod with him on the interview so I could hear the EVP. It was a chilling recording, and the voice on the tape sounded like that of a young man or boy. APS felt that Merrimack was one of the most haunted places in North Alabama.

During our interview, I also spoke to Leilani about Merrimack's history. Unlike most haunted places, Merrimack's history is not painted with death or tragedy. There were no terrible accidents in its darkened corners or horrible deaths in its shadows. The things that usually lead to hauntings are absent in the merry hall and are instead replaced by stories of parties, banquets and games. Leilani told me that spirits often return to places they were attached to in life. If this were true, it would make sense that many spirits would crowd Merrimack Hall since it was so important to so many people in life.

THE SPECTERS OF
SPACE CAMP

The U.S. Space and Rocket Center is the embodiment of a major historical shift in North Alabama. In the 1940s, North Alabama was witnessing the end of an era. The massive cotton and textile mills that had gained a foothold in the antebellum period and defined Alabama life for almost one hundred years were beginning to shut down, and they left a void behind them. In Huntsville Alabama, the Dallas Mill and other mills were a way of life, and their closure left many locals wondering what could possibly fill the hole left behind.

No one could have foreseen that the change North Alabama needed would come in the form of a German scientist who had designed some of the most dangerous missiles used by the Germans in World War II. Werner Von Braun is considered to be the preeminent engineer of the twentieth century. In Germany, he designed the deadly V-2 missile, the first long-range missile. It was also the first man-made machine to be launched into space. Von Braun and his colleagues were brought to the United States as part of the then top-secret operation paperclip. The agenda behind this operation was to acquire Germany's top scientists and bring them to the United States before they could be acquired by the Soviet Union.

Von Braun stayed at several bases before he was finally moved to Huntsville, Alabama, in 1950. However, it was Huntsville, Alabama, that

The Space and
Rocket Center.

Von Braun would finally call home, and he would transform it into a completely different city. Stationed at Redstone Arsenal, Von Braun was instrumental in the design of the Redstone missile, the first nuclear ballistic missile in the United States. Despite Von Braun's work on missiles, it was his dream to take man to the moon. He worked on the missiles because it was his job, but his passion always lay among the stars. Von Braun worked hard to make his dream a reality. He navigated his career in the United States carefully so that he would eventually be able to realize his dream of taking a man to the moon. His dream was finally made possible when NASA's Marshall Space Flight Center was put at Redstone Arsenal and Von Braun was named director. Working at Marshall Space Flight Center,

Von Braun went on to become the architect of the Saturn V rocket, which made it possible for the United States to put a man on the moon.

Von Braun's work changed everything. His work made it possible for the Americans to leap ahead of the Soviet Union in the arms race and in the space race. His work also put Huntsville, Alabama, on the map and changed the culture of this once small Alabama town forever.

In order to support the work of Von Braun and his colleagues, the arsenal began developing the Huntsville area as a center for the burgeoning aerospace industry. Aerospace and electrical engineers came from around the country to join the famous team and help the United States push forward in the space race that had become an epic competition in the cold war era. In the midst of this massive influx of population and jobs, Von Braun developed a vision of a new Huntsville. He developed a vision of Huntsville, Alabama, as the center of the aerospace world that would draw engineers and tourists from around the world.

To support his vision, Von Braun proposed the revolutionary idea of building a space museum in Huntsville to draw tourists. The local government of the time liked the idea but was unwilling to set the money aside. So the idea was put before the state legislature to find the financial support necessary. The legislature put it to a popular vote. The people of Alabama joined together to fight for this museum. Led by local Alabama heroes like University of Alabama football coach Bear Bryant, the people were able to win the popular vote by a landslide, and the U.S. Space and Rocket Center opened in Huntsville, Alabama, in 1970.

Since that time, Huntsville has gone from a tiny town of 20,000 to a burgeoning community of over 200,000, and it is still growing. It wasn't just Huntsville's population that changed. Its entire culture changed. The once southern town had evolved into a multicultural community that was drawing its residents from a global community of engineers and rocket scientists, and more and more highly educated professionals were coming to support the community of engineers swarming to Alabama. The blue-collar mill-working Huntsville was gone. In its place was a city that had the highest education level and socioeconomic status in the Southeast.

But Von Braun's vision wasn't complete. He wanted to make science and math exciting for children, and he wanted to change the way children looked at these subjects. At the time Von Braun proposed space camp, there was simply nothing else like it. It was a stellar success. Space camp opened its doors in 1982, and by 1986, it was so popular that a movie was made about it. The 1986 movie *Space Camp* was a box office hit, and even more children came to this novel new camp, which made science and space exciting and let them literally reach for the stars.

Today, children come from China, Australia, Taiwan and all over the world to learn how to be astronauts. Space camp has special programs for the vision and hearing impaired. One space camp employee shared a touching story with me about a little deaf girl who had never known she had a future. She had come to space camp as part of a special program for the hearing impaired. For the first time in her life, she was around other people with the same disability she had. She had never known any other deaf people, and she had been raised to believe that her handicap would make it impossible for her to ever achieve much in life. One day, this employee found the little girl crying and asked her why she was weeping. She said it was because she was so amazed to see grown hearing impaired people succeeding in the world. Her trip to space camp had changed her entire perception of the world, and she was weeping because, for the first time in her life, she had hope. She could grow up to be anything she wanted to be, even an astronaut. Her visit to space camp had changed her life. She's not the only one. Three current astronauts can count themselves among the legions of space camp alumni, and hundreds more alumni have gone on to have successful careers in the aerospace industry.

One might wonder why such a place as the U.S. Space and Rocket Center, a celebration of science and the modern world, would be rumored to be filled with ghosts. The first stories I heard about ghosts in space camp were nothing but rumors. They were tall tales spread by people who had never seen or heard ghosts. They were stories of explosions and unexplained deaths, of monstrous construction accidents that set the rocket center on fire and sent people screaming to a fiery death.

These stories were not true, but they took me to the U.S. Space and Rocket Center in search of their source. I spoke to several people anonymously, both present and past employees, and I found that the truth was far more interesting than the rumors. The only death to happen at the rocket center was the death of a construction worker who was painting the Saturn V in 1999. He was rushing, and he fell off some scaffolding and died. He's not the one haunting the space center, however.

HAB1.

Most of the ghost stories surrounding the space and rocket center seem to be focused on the area called HAB1. HAB1 is the human habitat area, where some of the campers reside during their stay at space camp. This futuristic-looking structure is the source of much of the seemingly harmless paranormal activity that takes place here. Within its silver walls, employees describe odd sounds, opening and closing doors, strange orbs of light and the sound of voices. Those who have walked around outside HAB1 describe the sounds of children playing and laughing, even at night when all the children are gone.

I spoke to one employee who told me something he said few knew. He said that the land behind the space and rocket center is owned by Redstone Arsenal. When the arsenal purchased the land, a family lived there. The condition upon which the family sold the land was that the arsenal would leave their family cemetery intact. This cemetery still stands in the forest behind HAB1. He also said that a little farther into the woods, slightly to the other side of HAB1, lies another cemetery. This cemetery was left intact because it holds the bones of what he called "Paylo" Indians. He spelled this for me as P-A-L-E-O.

I researched these mysterious Paleo-Indians and found something so obvious that I missed it at first. The term "Paleo" refers to something that is ancient. So Paleo-Indians doesn't refer to a tribe of Indians at all but to a time period in which the very first Americans inhabited the North American continent. The Paleo-Indian cemetery behind space camp is an ancient cemetery that dates back to the very first inhabitants of the Tennessee Valley.

My anonymous source believes that these two cemeteries are the sources of all the strange activity in HAB1. He and another employee I spoke with agree that this would explain why so much of the activity at space camp seems to occur outside the HAB1. The laughter, the voices and the lights have all been seen behind HAB1, in a place where two old cemeteries meet beside the gateway to the modern world.

This does not explain why some sources report seeing things and hearing noises in the U.S. Space and Rocket Center. Although these occurrences seem to be much less common, I spoke to one individual who thought that Von Braun himself might still wander the halls of his beloved space museum. This source thought Von Braun loved the space museum so deeply that he might have returned to it, even in death.

THE POTTER'S FIELD
PRESENCE

.Ⅰn the south of Huntsville, buried deep in the suburbs behind an ocean
of houses so thick you wouldn't even know it is there, there is a potter's
field. This potter's field is surrounded by backyard fences and is filled
with trees and thick undergrowth. It is completely hidden from all but
those who live with their backyards pressed up against it. The houses
pressed up against the potter's field are small and cozy looking. Many of
the front doors are open, inviting guests to come and visit. If you knock,
their residents will come and greet you congenially, with a pleasant smile
and a little story. A few of them will talk about the potter's field. They
complain about the teenagers who cut through their lawns to get to it, but
other than that, they are very tight-lipped.

I walked back to this little potter's field on an overcast day. A potter's field
is a burial place for paupers, criminals and unknown persons. Historically,
the first known potter's field was Aceldama, or "field of blood," a barren
place near Jerusalem. According to the Bible, the term was originally used
by potters, who called the burial ground Aceldama because it was bought
with the blood money paid Judas. Judas hanged himself after he betrayed
Jesus, and the money he was given was returned to the treasury. The treasury
used the funds to buy a field to bury strangers in because it did not want to
use blood money for anything else. Thus, the first potter's field was a field of

The potter's field.

blood. As you wander through the anonymous graves in this small field, you can't help but think of the legend. This was certainly a field of strangers.

The story of Huntsville's potter's field came to me from a woman, Sherry, who had grown up in a house next to the field. She remembers the house well, and when she talks about it she shudders a little. As soon as she moved into her home, strange things began to happen. Odd noises woke the family in the middle of the night. Lights went on and off. The family dog went crazy and began barking at nothing. It was clear that there was something wrong with the house.

It was Sherry's sister who saw the worst of the haunting. She was visited nightly by the ghost of a woman in olden-style dress. The ghost came and stood over her while she slept; if she woke up, she awoke to the eyes of a ghost staring down at her. Night after night this happened until the little girl could find no rest.

Although the ghost preferred Sherry's little sister, it also visited other family members. Some nights it came to visit Sherry, and although she didn't sense any malevolence in the ghost, she couldn't get to sleep knowing that the spirits of the dead were in her room. Sherry remembers one particular night when she was getting ready for work and the ghost turned off her music. Sherry turned the stereo back on. The ghost turned it off again. After this went on for a few minutes, Sherry called out and asked the ghost to stop. The ghost appeared to leave Sherry and her stereo alone.

Because of all the activity in the house, Sherry and her family looked into the field behind their house. They found out that the potter's field behind their house had belonged to a group of sharecroppers who had lived there over a century earlier. It had been many years since they had left the area, leaving only their dead behind. When the developers began building the neighborhood, they realized that they could not move or touch the small graveyard because they couldn't find the next of kin of any of those buried there. Most of the tombstones were in such ill repair that they couldn't even identify those who had been buried there. The potter's field had to remain, so the developers built around the graveyard. They left the small plot and put backyards right up against the gravestones. The houses are so tightly wrapped around the graveyard that you can't even walk to it without cutting through someone's yard. In fact, Sherry heard rumors that some of the houses may have been inadvertently placed right on top of some of the unmarked graves.

It was obvious to Sherry and her family that this was the source of their problems. Sherry's mother grew panicked and desperate, so she called a priest to come and exorcise the house. The priest came, and the ritual was done. The priest went from room to room blessing the house and praying. The ritual seemed to work, and for a while the girls slept peacefully.

A year later, construction began on the other side of the potter's field. New houses were built, and the soil was disturbed. The haunting returned with a vengeance. Doors opened and shut. Banging filled the house. No one in the house could sleep. Ghosts returned to the beds of both girls, and the women decided it was time to leave.

It has been many years since Sherry lived in the house by the potter's field. But she'll never forget the spirits that still wander its darkened grounds. She'll never forget the faces of the ghosts that came into their house and kept them awake at night.

THE HEADLESS GHOSTS
OF FERRAR HOUSE

There is a ghost story in Limestone County. The story says that a man named Perrin Farrar built a house off Snake Road. He and his two beautiful daughters lived there happily. It was their home, and they wanted for nothing.

According to legend, one dark night, while everyone was sleeping, a man snuck into their home. He crept up to the two sleeping beauties and cut their lovely heads from their bodies. According to the legend, the beauties never left the house. Each night at about eleven o'clock, at least one headless woman in white can be seen gliding through the house where she was so brutally murdered.

I have seen and heard this story in several places. Two versions of the story were published in a book by Alan Brown called *The Face in the Window*. The first story in this book is a firsthand account of an experience a visitor to the area had with the white lady of Ferrar House. This individual says that a woman came up to him and then vanished. The second account in this book is really just a retelling of the legend itself. This story tells of an old house on Snake Road, built in 1854. The house is dark and dilapidated. According to legend, blood still stains the floors. The house is filled with ghosts. The tale describes the headless ghost that is seen coming down the stairs of Ferrar House late at night. It tells of her bloodstained dress and the grisly stump that occupies the space where her head should be. In the author's note, he indicates that both accounts were disregarded as legend not based in fact.

Other people with whom I have discussed this story have told me the tale with a wink and smile. It is clearly a story that is told and not believed. They think it is a little bit of southern folklore that is fun to pass on. It's a story that is best told late at night over a roaring campfire.

The truth, however, is that there was a Perrin Ferrar. Perrin was the child of Stephen Farrar and Elizabeth Rice and was born in 1793. Perrin married Rebecca Freeman in 1830 in Lawrence County. Together they had eight children: four daughters, Martha, Sarah, Mary and Louisa; and four sons, Holman R., William J., Robert L. and Joseph C. Perrin secured a homestead in Limestone County and moved his entire family there. His first home was built on Davis Road. Many members of the Farrar family moved to Alabama around this time, and the land was checkered with their homesteads. In truth, there were many Perrin Ferrars. It seems to have been a very common name in the landscape of old Alabama.

The house on Davis Road is probably where the murders took place. Records show that Perrin did have two daughters who died in this house in their youth. His daughters Louisa and Sally both died in the house on Davis Road. Mary died later in childbirth. The house on Snake Road wasn't built until after the murders. It was built in 1854, and the Ferrar family stayed there.

The Farrar, or "Farrow," Cemetery is located close to the Snake Road house on Highway 72 in Athens. Many members of the Ferrar family rest there. The cemetery has suffered some desecration, and many of the tombstones have been pushed into a ditch. This makes it impossible to know the names of everyone who is buried in this old family graveyard.

The girls may not have been murdered in the house that so many think is haunted, but it seems possible that their ghosts stayed with their family. They traveled with them, haunting them. They kept to the family they loved so deeply.

THE HAUNTING OF HUNTSVILLE DEPOT

Many have said that the Huntsville Depot is the most haunted place in North Alabama. They say that there are more ghosts at this old train station than any place else in the region. It is hard to imagine that there are ghosts at the depot when you pull up to it. It is a bright place, and children run through the grassy areas just outside the building. There is a caboose for birthday parties and a sandbox. A small trolley runs in circles around the grounds carrying giggling children. When you step into the depot itself, the atmosphere changes, and the building seems dark even on the sunniest day. The stairs are askew, and all of the angles are wrong. Animatronic figures stare out at you with glassy eyes, and for those who feel such things, there is a sense that there is something present in the building.

The Huntsville Depot is the oldest surviving railroad station in Alabama. It is also one of the oldest railroad stations in the United States. The depot was completed in 1860 and was part of the Memphis and Charleston Railroad, the first to connect the Mississippi River to the Atlantic Ocean. This railroad became a major artery for the South and was the only one that unified the South. The depot was built to be more impressive and elegant than most depots on the line because it was also the Eastern Division headquarters. It was built to be a central connecting element for the railroads of the South. Evidence of this can be seen in its size

The Huntsville Depot.

and elegance. It is three stories high and is filled with large rooms and refined spaces. Dark, polished hardwood floors run through the depot, and beautiful banisters and details fill every room.

For obvious reasons, the Memphis and Charleston Railroad was of critical importance during the Civil War. It served as a means to transport Confederate soldiers, ammunition and supplies between the Southern states. As part of this critical Southern link, the Huntsville Depot became of central importance to the Confederacy. Huntsville didn't fully understand how important the depot had become. In fact, Huntsville was taken entirely by surprise when it was targeted by Union forces in an effort to cut off the South's supply lines. On April 11, 1862, General Mitchell led 6,000 Union soldiers into Huntsville, Alabama. The general was subtle in his attack. The soldiers were dressed in civilian clothes, so they went almost unnoticed. They attacked early in the morning, before the sun had risen to wake the earliest of risers. They took the town completely by surprise and were able to capture 159 soldiers on a train from Shiloh. They took the depot and

Huntsville virtually without fight. Huntsville had been unprepared, and all the men of fighting age were gone. The Union's attack was both efficient and unexpected.

For the rest of the Civil War, Union forces occupied the depot and Huntsville. The depot itself was used as an office building, and the third floor was used for prisoners. Old train cars were converted into hospitals for the wounded prisoners. During the time the depot was used as a prison, the prisoners occupied themselves by decorating the walls with graffiti. That graffiti still remains, covered in plastic, as a reminder of the men who spent many long days imprisoned in the depot.

When the war ended in 1865, the Union soldiers abandoned the depot and left Huntsville behind. Huntsville wasn't the same, however. The war took its toll on the entire South, and Huntsville and the depot were no exceptions to this rule. The Memphis and Charleston Railroad was closed for good and was eventually bought out by the Southern Railroad.

Until 1968, the Huntsville Depot remained a vital link in the Southern Railroad and witnessed many important events in North Alabama. It remained a transportation hub for the Southeast and saw the comings and goings of generations of weary travelers. As an important hub of transportation, the Huntsville Depot witnessed the ebb and flow of history in the region. Teddy Roosevelt came through town on a whistle-stop campaign and spoke to the citizens of Huntsville from his train at the depot. During both world wars, teary-eyed wives, children and mothers waved farewell to their beloveds as they traveled away to war. In 1950, the team of Dr. Werner Von Braun's German scientists passed through the terminal, foreshadowing the demise of the old depot and the rebirth of Huntsville as a central player in the aerospace industry. The last train came through the depot in 1968.

The Huntsville Depot was abandoned but not forgotten. When plans were made to demolish the building, Huntsville residents petitioned city hall, and the Huntsville Depot was placed on the National Registry of Historic Places. The Huntsville Depot was restored and transformed into a museum of history. It became part of the Earlyworks Museum Complex, which includes Constitution Village. Today, the depot is as beautiful as ever. It is surrounded by old train cars and fire trucks. The grounds that were once occupied by Union troops are now covered in soft green grass and pretty sandboxes. A caboose in front of the depot is filled with happy children celebrating birthdays.

It isn't surprising that the depot is haunted. It has been a focal point of Alabama history for a century and a half, and many ghost stories clutter the grounds and the halls of the historic Huntsville Depot. Crowds of visitors and employees have shared ghost stories as numerous as the years the depot has stood in Alabama soil. Visitors have reported seeing a face staring out of the second-story window that looks down on the field below. Other visitors have reported feeling a sense of dread when they approach the dark and eerie vault that sits in the back of the second floor. Some say there is a cold spot near the vault, and others say that the door to the vault opens and closes on its own. Some visitors have seen the ghost of a railroad employee wandering the tracks of the old station.

The haunted vault.

I spoke with one of the employees of the depot. Mr. Winter Forest told me the details of the many legends that seem to spring up out of the shadows. Mr. Forest wasn't sure he believed all the ghost stories that surround the old train station, but he had seen a lot of people come through who did. According to Mr. Forest, there was an employee who worked at the depot thirty years ago who had an encounter with one of the spirits there. Her office had been on the second floor, and she had been working when she felt a presence, as if something was watching her. She turned around and saw a dark specter standing directly behind her. She was petrified and unable to respond to the dark spirit; then she felt a blast of cold air. She left and never came back. She was transferred to another location.

Mr. Forest also told me about one of the more popular legends associated with the depot. The legend says that a little girl was murdered and buried somewhere around the depot. The girl's body has never been found, but legend says that this little girl still wanders the grounds of the depot at night. She wanders the depot looking for her way home.

One psychic I spoke with said she definitely sensed a very strong presence on the second floor of the building. She said it was a quiet spirit that was often irritated by the commotion and bedlam that surround the depot. She said it is unhappy when there are too many people around, and it prefers the quiet times when the depot is silent and empty.

Other visitors to the depot have reported seeing strange lights on the third floor and feeling a presence. One psychic who came to the depot said that the haunting of the depot seemed centered on the vault on the second floor. Another psychic indicated that the depot is filled with more than one ghost; there seems to be a cluster of ghosts present. This psychic described the depot as a waiting place for the spirits of the dead, where many spirits congregate before they cross over to the other side. According to this psychic, no one ghost story created this incredibly haunted location. The depot belongs to the spirits of many.

THE WINSTON HOUSE

The ghosts of Winston House find their ancestry and origins in the founding of the nation. They are old ghosts with distinguished genealogy and important and influential descendants. They are some of the oldest ghosts in the state. Tracing their origins is like tracing the history of the state of Alabama itself. They are the ghosts of the very first men to fight for this country and make it their own. It is no wonder that they are reluctant to leave the land that they would come to define.

Winston House was built for the grandson of Captain Anthony Winston and his wife, Keziah Walker Jones. Captain Winston was a cousin of Dolly Madison and Patrick Henry. He was a member of the Virginia Convention of 1775 and a gallant captain in the Revolutionary army. He served in the militia and was quickly promoted. Captain Winston was a Virginia man from Buckingham County.

It took years for Captain Winston to move his family from his home in Virginia, where he fought to found this nation, to Tuscumbia, Alabama. Captain Winston moved westward to claim the land that was given to him for his service in the Revolutionary War. He had a comfortable plantation in Virginia, and free land was the only thing that would move him away from it. He moved to Wilson County, Tennessee, in 1801. It was no easy task for him to move to Tennessee. He had to move his two brothers, his brother-in-law, his children, his wife, household goods and slaves. The family must have been restless because they moved about a great deal over the next few years. They moved from Lebanon, Tennessee, to Nashville and then on to Huntsville, Alabama. In Alabama, they engaged in land speculation and business.

In 1812, Captain Winston's son Anthony was asked by General Andrew Jackson to help raise a company of cavalry. Two of the captain's sons, John Jones and Anthony, both fought in the War of 1812. They were with the Second Tennessee Regiment. Together, they fought in the Battles of Tallushatchee, Talladega and Horseshoe Bend, defending General Jackson. After the war, more land became available to the west, and Colonel Anthony Winston took charge of the family affairs and moved his family again to follow the land.

Colonel Anthony acquired thousands of acres of land around the Tuscumbia area. The Winston family was very tightknit. Captain Winston and his wife were the first of the family to be buried in the Winston Cemetery. He died in 1828. The family had stayed together through two wars and four relocations. Just prior to his father's death, in 1833, William Winston completed the Georgian-style Winston House. The house is located less than a quarter of a mile from the Winston Cemetery, which has kept the family's dead for generations.

This was just the beginning for the Winston family. The Winston family would go on to shape Alabama history. One of their descendants would become Governor John Anthony Winston, the first native-born governor of Alabama. Another descendant would go on to be Edmund Winston Pettus, a senator in the U.S. Congress. Another descendant would become Governor John J. Pettus, a governor of Mississippi.

William Winston was an impressive man. He was the father of a governor, father-in-law to another Alabama governor and grandfather of Maud Lindsey, who was famous for her children's books. The Winston family seemed born to make history, and the William Winston House was the family home of this amazing family.

The Winston House is beautiful, like you would expect it to be. It is the largest standing antebellum house in Tuscumbia. It has a winding staircase, eight fireplaces and a log kitchen. Outside, the house is in perfect condition.

The red brick lines maintain their perfect symmetry. It almost seems new it is so well kept.

In 1948, the house and the land it sat on were sold to the City of Tuscumbia. This action ensured the house's position of importance in the community. The house was purchased as the site for the new campus of Deshler High School. The original campus sat on land that had been given to the city by Major David Deshler. The school was named for his son, James Deshler, who was killed leading the charge at the Battle of Chickamauga.

Today, the house is still part of the Deshler High School campus. A look at the school's website gives you a view of the house surrounded by the rest of the high school. High school students haven't missed the importance of having this beautiful house on their campus. The high school even has its own paranormal society, which has investigated the ghostly activity surrounding the house.

According to legend, the house is haunted by at least two ghosts. The first ghost is the ghost of William Winston himself. People claim to have seen him standing at the top of the stairs or wandering the halls of the old house. Those who believe these stories say that William has been unable to let go of the house he loved so passionately in life. They say that even in death he remains in his home and that he intends to remain there forever.

One Tuscumbia resident described the Winston House as the location of many walking ghosts. She said that on dark nights, white-clad figures are said to float and rise through the air. She says that there is a white lady in the house that can be seen walking up the stairs and that these phenomena are only visible for a fleeting moment; if you turn away, they will vanish.

According to tradition, the fleeting moments offer a glimpse into the true nature of this most historical and haunted house.

THE GHOST OF
WOODLAND HOSPITAL

Woodland Medical Center was a privately owned hospital located in Cullman, Alabama. Founded as Doctor's Hospital in 1974, the medical facility has changed owners several times over the course of its history. Woodland Hospital is reflective of any typical North Alabama hospital in the sense that it has been bought and sold and changed names and faces over the years. The medical field in North Alabama is all about money, and companies come and go in their desire to find a financially viable situation. In its final days, Woodland Hospital was bought out by Capella Incorporated. Capella Incorporated owns Hartselle Medical Center and Parkway Medical Center, also located in North Alabama.

In its golden years, Woodland Hospital was known throughout the region for its quality of care. It had over one hundred physicians and staff serving twenty-three fields of medicine. Like most hospitals, Woodland saw its share of suffering. Anyone who has ever worked in a hospital knows that hospitals are primarily places of sorrow. Most of the time, if you are in the hospital, you are not happy to be there. If you are watching a loved one slowly fade away in a hospital, your cry mingles with the cries of countless others who have stood at the feet of their beloveds' beds and watched death reach out for them.

Woodland added to the general sorrow associated with illness and death by placing a psychiatric ward in the hospital. The hospital didn't only witness

Woodland Hospital.

death, sickness and tragedy but also served as a place where those who had lost their minds could come and try to regain their sanity. Connoisseurs of ghost stories will tell you that psychiatric hospitals are some of the most haunted places on earth. They house people who have seen so much suffering that they find life is no longer bearable. They are the last resort for the desperate, the forgotten and the lost. These places are imprinted with the lingering emotions of those who have lost all desire to carry on and those who have been driven to violence by their own inner demons.

Despite all this, Woodland Hospital was a busy place and respected in its community. In fact, this suffering is nothing extraordinary in the medical community; it is how a hospital deals with such sorrow that defines it. Apparently, Woodland Medical Center and its staff dealt well with the tragedy in the hospital walls. It was well known as a place of healing and help. It was described by the *Cullman Times* as being an exemplary hospital and a comforting place to take your loved ones when they are ill. The paper added that for thirty-five years, the people of Woodland Medical Center dedicated themselves to providing the highest quality of healthcare to the residents of Cullman County and the surrounding areas. Through their inviting atmosphere and dedication to patient care, Woodland earned a reputation as a great place to work and receive excellent treatment.

Woodland was a popular hospital, but it was not without its secrets. I have heard from many of the staff members who made Woodland Hospital their home that the ghosts that wandered the halls of this typical hospital were everything but quiet. The ghostly occurrences that happened became so common that the staff turned the supernatural activity into a kind of joke. They laughed about the call lights that went on and off on their own and told jokes about the doors that opened and closed without provocation.

The irony of the hospital is that despite all the suffering and anguish that went on inside the building, the ghost came from outside the building. Homer was not a patient of the hospital. He was an old man who loved his home. Before Woodland was built, Homer owned all the land that the hospital was built on. He had spent his life in his home on the land. People had tried to buy his land on multiple occasions. The location was in the center of town and was easily accessible. Homer wasn't interested in selling. He wanted to keep his land. When the hospital started making him offers, Homer dug in his heels and refused to give up his home. It wasn't until he died that construction could begin on the hospital.

But even in death, Homer didn't like the hospital that was built over his home. He hated its presence and hated those who had destroyed his house to build the hospital. He was angry and bitter, and his spirit lingered, adding to the suffering of the living. The haunting became part of daily life at Woodland Hospital. Homer wasn't a particularly aggressive ghost. He made a lot of commotion that was witnessed by nurses and visitors. He seemed to be particularly active near the psychiatric ward and kept the staff on their toes there. He liked to flush the toilets on this floor.

There was one tree in particular that the staff liked to congregate around to smoke and talk. One nurse told me that when she would stand out at the tree and look back at the hospital, she could see lights going on and off. She knew there was no one in those rooms, but the lights still flickered.

Staff members have also told me that Homer tended to follow death. He was more active right before a patient died. Ghostly activity would increase in rooms where patients were about to die. He predicted death

The long hall.

and often became much louder and more noticeable before and after a patient's demise.

On July 15, 2009, Cullman Regional Medical Center finalized agreements between it and Capella to buy out Woodland Medical Center. According to the *Cullman Times*, on July 15 the hospital was shut down, and operations were consolidated and moved to Cullman Regional Medical Center. This decision was not based on ghost stories or flickering lights but on financial necessity. The region simply wasn't big enough to sustain two large hospitals, and consolidation was the only reasonable answer to the dilemma.

The hospital closed its doors, and the staff was shuffled off to Woodland's sister hospitals in Decatur and Hartselle, where many of the nurses and staff still work today. Although they have moved away from Woodland Medical Center, they haven't forgotten Homer and eagerly share their stories about their brushes with this phantom.

Those nurses who remained until the very end tell darker stories. After the hospital shut its doors to patients, some of the staff remained to clean out the hospital and take care of paperwork. The electric wiring was taken out of many of the rooms to be used in other facilities. It was during this time that Homer seemed to go crazy. Throughout the hospital, call lights that no longer had electricity went on and off. Room lights flickered, and doors slammed.

Two former employees told me one story that sent chills up my spine. Susan had worked at Woodland for many years and knew Homer well, but she wasn't prepared for what happened on one of her last nights there. She was gathering paperwork and was walking toward the file room. As she walked toward the door, a sharp chill gripped her, and she shuddered. The door she was walking toward opened and shut suddenly in front of her.

Confused, Susan turned and looked around. She saw one of her friends and co-workers running away from her. When she spoke with her friend later, the other woman described seeing a full-formed phantom man walk through Susan, cross the hall and open and shut the door Susan was heading toward. Susan still shivers when she thinks about it.

Woodland Hospital is empty now. There is no more electricity, and it has no more patients. It is quiet. I went to Woodland and peeked in the

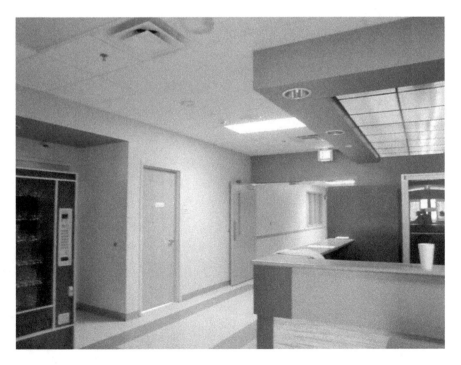

Two faces in the glass.

windows. I was even able to step inside for a few minutes. I saw nothing in the hospital. It was empty and cold. I snapped a few pictures. In one of the pictures, I could see my face reflected in the glass in front of me. I could see my head and shoulders. I could also see someone standing behind me, but I was alone, and the hospital was empty. I have to wonder if Homer came to say hello. The campus is for sale, and Capella hopes that it will be purchased for use as an outpatient facility of some kind, but for now Woodland belongs to Homer.

HELL'S GATES

It's not easy to find Hell's Gates. They aren't where you would expect to find them. They aren't buried in a tangled mass of thorns in some darkened forest or lost in the fog of an unapproachable swamp. They are located in plain sight and are easily missed because they are in such a picturesque and serene location. They sneak up on you, and before you know it, you have driven past them without even knowing they were there.

Green Mountain is located in Huntsville, Alabama, on the south side of the city. It is a popular place for young lovers to take a stroll or for mothers to take their children to play. It is most well known for the Madison County Nature Trail, a seventy-two-acre park that was completed in 1975. The trail meanders around a lovely lake filled with geese and turtles. If you take the path around the lake, you will pass picture-perfect wildflowers carefully labeled with their genus and specie. You'll pass over handmade bridges and walk past the Champion elm, which is the oldest elm in Alabama. At the end of the trail, you'll come to a secluded chapel that brings to mind images of times long ago, when the settlers of this area must have met in nature, beneath the trees. There are streams and waterfalls along the way, and if you are quiet and careful, the occasional playful fox will sneak up and watch you from the shelter of the trees.

Green Mountain is known as a peaceful place where friends and family gather to picnic and fish and be part of the serenity of nature. There are old log cabins on the mountains that remind hikers that they are part of history. Visitors leaving Green Mountain are usually at peace.

It is because of all this peace that Hell's Gates seem so out of place. On the drive down the mountain, you pass through lush forest, thick with kudzu. The forest here is so thick that it's difficult to see anything, but if you drive slowly, you'll see Hell's Gates out the right-hand side of your window. They are black and rusted and always closed. They are wrapped in kudzu and almost seem to be part of the trees bending around them.

With Hell's Gates, it's hard to separate legend from fact. Many people know the story of the gates, and many will swear they know someone who has seen the hellish apparition that is said to lurk behind the gates, but a rare few will say they've seen it themselves. Local legend says that if you go to the gates and pull up beside them and wait, a car will pull up behind you. The black car won't have any driver, but it will chase you, honking, down the mountain and vanish into the fog when you reach the bottom.

I investigated this legend, which is told mostly by teenagers. One adult I interviewed told me that he had tried to pull up beside the gates to study them. He said that as he got out of his car, a black car pulled up behind him and began honking loudly. At this point, he panicked and got in his car, fleeing down the mountain. He indicated that he didn't see the car vanish, but when he finally looked back, the car was gone. He also said he couldn't be sure that the car was in any way supernatural, as it was dark and he couldn't see if there was a driver. Supernatural or not, stories like these perpetuate the legend, and people continue to believe that dark forces lurk in the shadows of these gates.

I interviewed one local woman who told me an even more sinister story. According to her, she knew several people involved in Wicca when she was young. Her friends decided that Hell's Gates would be a good location to perform some of their rites because they thought there might be supernatural energy that could be drawn from this location. They parked their car and wandered into the woods behind the gates late at night. They built a huge fire and laid out all the equipment they would need for their ritual. Being teenagers, they also had several beers. Before they began, one of their friends snuck off into the darkness to use the bathroom. The other teens waited for hours, but their friend never returned. The entire story never reached the unfortunate teen's parents because none of the young people involved wanted to admit they had been doing Wiccan rituals and drinking beer in the woods in the middle of the night, so the young person was called a runaway. According to this witness, they never heard from their friend again.

Whether or not you believe the numerous stories about Hell's Gates, there is something ominous about the gates themselves. They are black and rusted and seem to guard nothing but the shadows. When you open them, they groan angrily as if they are protesting your presence. I journeyed to the gates on a bright winter day. I parked my car and walked into the area behind them where there is still evidence of the many young people who must go back there to build bonfires. There are also the remains of occult symbols and evidence of the occult activity that must take place behind the gates. I did not see any phantom car during my trip, and none of my photographs had any of the ghosts or demons that should be present to indicate paranormal activity. Still, the place sent shivers down my spine, and I was more than happy to leave when the time came.

THE DEMON IN THE DARK

Amy's new house was a dream come true. Amy and her husband had never imagined that they could afford such a beautiful and spacious home. They were on a tight budget, and when they started house hunting, they thought they would have to start at the bottom. The house they found seemed more like the top, and they counted themselves blessed to be able to afford a house that should have been out of their reach financially. The house had vaulted ceilings, recessed lighting and hardwood floors. It was in a good neighborhood with good schools.

Amy was thrilled to move into her new home. It was a rental with a buy option built into the rental agreement. Amy and her husband had every intention of buying the house. It was everything they wanted. They were happy and excited, and their lives seemed to be moving in the right direction.

They rented the house and began the process of moving in immediately. They unloaded their boxes with the joy that can only come from finding a happy home. Amy had no reason to expect that anything would go wrong. She was filled with hope and optimism for herself and her little family. At the time, she couldn't imagine much that could get in the way of her happiness.

It wasn't long before Amy began to notice something odd about the house. She was moving boxes into the bedroom and had to close a closet door to get through the hall. She closed the door and put some boxes in the

The Demon in the Dark.

room. As she walked back by, she noticed that the door was open again. Amy shrugged, assuming that she hadn't latched it tightly enough, and shut the door again, making sure it was latched. On her way back through the house, the door was open again. This continued throughout the day.

That night, as she slept, Amy felt uneasy in the house. She felt as if there was something wrong, but she didn't say anything because she didn't want to believe it. She didn't want to believe that anything could possibly be wrong with her dream house. So she ignored the strange feeling, and she ignored the door that opened on its own. She told herself it was some flaw in the house's structure and settled in to her new life in her new house.

The longer Amy and her husband stayed in the house, the more strange things began to happen. The TV turned itself off at eleven o'clock every night. One night, while she was watching TV, the TV shut off and a light bulb exploded in the bathroom. The bathroom light had been off, and Amy was alone. She felt shaken by the light bulb incident and replaced the bulb. The bulb exploded again. Amy changed the bulb several times, and finally she had to call an electrician. The electrician gave her no answers. There was no reason for the light bulb to explode, and he couldn't even understand how it had exploded when the light switch was off.

Amy began spending more and more time alone in the house. Her husband took the third shift at work, and it seemed like he was gone all the time. Amy's best friend had come to visit several times, but her friend indicated that she felt uncomfortable in Amy's house and didn't want to be there. Amy had to coax her friend into coming into the house, and even then, her friend refused to stay long. Her friend sensed that there was something wrong with the house. She wouldn't elaborate on her feelings; she just didn't want to be in the house.

The occurrences continued and seemed to escalate as time went on. The TV always went off at 11:00 p.m., and light bulbs throughout the house exploded from time to time. Amy's stepson came to stay with her now and again, and he heard her calling to him, even when the house was empty.

Finally, Amy decided to investigate. She asked the neighbors about the house and gained little useful information. The house had been a rental for some time, and families moved in and out of the house very quickly. The neighbors said that three families had moved in and out of the house in the three months prior to Amy's arrival. Knowing this did nothing to calm Amy's frayed nerves. She was also able to find out that the closet door that refused to stay shut had once belonged to a bedroom.

Amy and her husband were determined to make the house work, despite Amy's ill ease. Amy's husband was working more and more, so he didn't see

Amy's house.

the problems. He made light of the incidents when Amy explained them to him. He was a skeptic and couldn't believe that something supernatural existed in their house. He wanted to stay, and Amy still loved the idea of her beautiful new home.

After a year had passed, they decided to get a dog. Amy's stepson wanted a dog, and Amy liked the idea of having company in the house when she was alone. As soon as the dog stepped in the house, he started barking and snarling. The dog went crazy. It never stopped barking and ran laps around the house. It dug into the floor and created such a constant commotion that they could no longer stand the noise. The animal had to go, despite the family's attachment to it. They gave the dog away, and Amy was left alone in the house again.

It was shortly after this that Amy's husband began to realize that there might be something wrong with the house. One night, while the two were sleeping, they were both awakened by heavy footsteps outside their bedroom. Her husband got up to investigate the footsteps. He followed them around the house in vain and finally climbed back into bed. When he got back into bed, the couple lay in quiet terror as the door opened. The footsteps approached the bed and then turned and left. After that, the couple agreed that there was something in the house.

It was shortly after that night that things began to get much worse for Amy. Amy began to suffer from night terrors in which horrible monsters tormented her. She would wake up in the morning covered with scratches and bruises. Amy tried everything. She put mittens and gloves on her hands at night and wore long-sleeved pajamas, but the cuts were getting worse, and Amy was becoming terrified. Every moment she spent in the house was turning into a nightmare, and she couldn't even find peace in sleep.

At this point, the couple knew they had to leave, but leaving is never as easy as it seems. They had to save their money and finish out the year left on their lease before they could go. Amy could no longer sleep alone in the house, and she started staying up on the couch until her husband got off work in the middle of the night. After a while, that wasn't even enough, and Amy had to go stay with her parents until her husband came home.

The nightly footsteps persisted and became so loud on one occasion that Amy had to stop her husband from calling the police. One night, Amy returned from her parents' house a little too early and found herself alone in the house. She called a friend to keep her company on the phone until her husband got home. Left alone, Amy began to hear noises, and she followed them through the house until she entered a bedroom. She turned on the light, and just as the light bulb exploded, she saw a black form hunched over in the back of the room. Amy dropped the phone and ran to the car. She spent the rest of the night at her parents' house.

As things got worse, Amy's scratches and bruises spread from her arms to her back. Her fear became overwhelming, and even Amy's husband was awakened in the middle of the night to sounds coming from the living room. He thought he was hearing a party, but when he went to look everything was quiet. In a moment of desperation, Amy called her friend to do a cleansing. Her friend went from room to room reading from the Bible and anointing the house. Amy was sure that the anointing would work. It had to work, because she couldn't stand the haunting any longer. The anointing was completely ineffectual. In fact, it seemed to make things worse. The ghost became more aggressive than ever. The cuts and bruises got worse, and Amy got to the point where she was spending more time in her parents' home than in her own. Amy and her husband wanted to wait and at least salvage some of the money they had put into the house, but things had escalated to the point where they had become unbearable.

Finally, Amy and her husband gave up. They couldn't take the fear anymore. They couldn't take the anxiety. Amy was afraid to sleep at night and could no longer be alone in the house. She was haunted by nightmares, and her body hurt with the scratches and bruises that came two or three times a week. They packed up their belongings and left all the money they'd invested in the house behind. Amy and her husband now live in an apartment and are still saving up to buy their dream house. Amy can finally sleep through the night, and all the scratches on her arms have healed. Amy showed me the scars on her arms. She called me because she needed to talk to someone about the horror that had tormented her for years. Amy has moved on, but sometimes she still wakes up from nightmares that she is trapped in that house with no way out. She is screaming and no one can hear her. Amy is safe from whatever bad spirit tortured her in the house of her dreams, but the haunting lives on in her nightmares.

THE LEGEND OF CRYBABY HOLLOW

The story of Crybaby Hollow is older than anyone can remember. It is a ghost story people have told so many times that it has become a legend. I've heard this story many times. It's been told to me by co-workers, friends and people I hardly know. The story changes with each telling. Even the location changes with the telling. Sometimes the name changes form. I've even heard it called Crybaby Holler. No matter what you call it, the haunting is the same. Somewhere on a lonely stretch of highway deep in rural Alabama, there is a place haunted by the ghost of a lost child. The road is always Highway 31. The ghost is always sad, and there is always crying. It is the crying that defines the haunting and the sense that somewhere on Highway 31, something horrible happened that left the ghost of a child or children trapped in the lonely netherworld in the woods by Crybaby Hollow.

The first person who told me about Crybaby Hollow said it was located just outside of Decatur between Decatur and Hartselle on Highway 31. He said that the haunting was ancient and that the hollow was located on a narrow bridge that passed over a small creek. According to this gentleman, the haunting is so old that it even predates the presence of Europeans in Alabama. When the Native Americans still ruled Alabama, a young woman was out foraging with her baby. She had been foraging in the area around Crybaby Hollow. She didn't know that the area around the hollow was prone

Crybaby Hollow.

to flash flooding, so she didn't panic when it started to rain. A flood came and swept her away. She survived, but her baby was lost in the rain. To this day, her baby haunts the hollow, forever searching for her mother and crying for help that will never come.

Another common version of this story gives the haunting slightly more recent origins. According to this legend, the ghost dates back to the first European settlers. The settlers were traveling by wagon across the harsh terrain of Alabama. At some point, one of the wheels was caught in a root and broke. This breakage threw the wagon off balance, and the baby that was sleeping in the back of the wagon slid out of the wagon and into the narrow creek. By the time anyone noticed the baby was gone, it was too late. The baby had already drowned and has remained in the creek ever since, haunting all those who pass by the ominous bridge.

A Decatur resident told me a simpler story. According to this legend, a young woman became pregnant out of wedlock. This was in the 1950s, and at that time she was shunned for her indiscretion and the pregnancy that followed. The young woman grew to hate the life growing within her, and when the baby was born she tossed it into the water by Crybaby Hollow. The baby died, but its ghost remains.

One final version of this story is the most disturbing and the most recent. According to another source I spoke with, a murderer tormented the Hartselle area in the 1940s. He killed a pregnant woman and a little boy. He threw the baby boy and the woman into the creek by Crybaby Hollow. Both apparitions still haunt the creek.

There are many other stories. In fact, it seems like every person I talk to has a different story to share about this haunted stretch of shadowy road. Most people regard this story as legend. They dismiss it, but I have spoken with several locals who insist that this legend is true. Although they may not agree on the story behind the haunting, several people have described having their car shaken by an unknown source when they stop on the narrow bridge off Highway 31. Another anonymous source insisted that he heard phantom wailing and found handprints on his car when he stopped. Others have told me that they have left candy bars on the side of the road, and when they returned, the candy was either gone or had been partially eaten.

The legend of Crybaby Hollow has the texture and tone of an urban legend. There is no way to verify any of these stories as true historically, and everyone knows a slightly different version of the story. The only way the story seems to differ from a typical urban legend is that there are many witnesses who insist they have actually seen the ghost themselves or had encounters with the ghost. I even spoke with one woman who claims to have photographed the infant's face reflected in the water beneath the bridge.

Blair Jett and his team at the Paranormal Research Alliance did a thorough investigation of the site. They did not find any conclusive evidence of a haunting at this location; however, they found many subjective signs of activity at the site. They heard ghostly moaning and disembodied voices, and one of the investigators described feeling something pressing on her chest. They got a significant amount of video footage from the location and did EVPs. If you watch their video, you can hear moaning in the distance during quiet moments.

THE GUARDIAN GHOST

Allison is a professional woman. She has a successful career and is respected in the community. She is smart, put together and well known for her good sense and wit. She is not the type of woman you would imagine believing in ghost stories. She seems far too practical to indulge in such stories. Yet the ghost of Allison's house came to her, and she is more than happy to share her experience over a glass of wine.

As soon as Allison stepped into the house, she knew there was something not right about it. She felt a presence immediately and knew that she would not be alone in the beautiful home. Allison, however, was never one to be intimidated by ghosts or goblins, so she bought the house and began to make it her own.

Allison was very happy with her purchase and started the long process of settling in. She cleaned out cupboards and unpacked boxes. She hung pictures and did all the normal things people do when they move in. There were no regrets. Even when she was sure there was something else lurking in the dark corners of her house, she was happy to be home. By the time she was settled into the house, the presence had made itself known to her. She caught her first glimpse of her new roommate while she was cleaning the bathroom floors. She paused in her work, looked up and saw the ghost that was to become part of her life. Allison describes the ghost as little more than a misty fog. It floated down the hall and vanished.

Allison is a woman with a good head on her shoulders, and she didn't allow the incident to bother her. She continued on with her life and grew accustomed to the idea that she was living with something not of this world. It wasn't long after that when the chandelier began to sway on its own, and Allison noticed other odd occurrences throughout the house. It was at this point that Allison became curious. If she was going to live with a ghost, she wanted to know what kind of ghost she was living with. She began to investigate her new friend. She went to the neighbors' houses and asked them about the previous owners of her lovely house.

For many years prior to Allison's purchase of the home in 2005, the house was occupied by an old woman and her daughter. The daughter was a loving and doting girl who took care of her mother for many years. They lived together and were an amiable pair. The daughter stayed with her mother until the hour of her death and cared for her lovingly until her last moments. Her mother's name was Judy, and the old woman died in her own bed of cancer in 1998. The neighbors all described Judy as a sweet and kind woman. They loved having both her and her daughter as their neighbor. No one could say a bad thing about either woman who had lived in the house.

Naturally, Allison was happy to find out that her new roommate was friendly, and she didn't think much more of it until sometime later, when she left her house in the middle of a storm to go visit a friend. She stayed with her friend for a while and then drove back home. The next day, Allison's friend called and told her that something odd was going on in her house. There were strange clanging noises and objects would move on their own. Allison went out to help her friend investigate. She found nothing out of the ordinary, and when she went home, the strange activity left with her. That night, Allison's house was filled with ghostly commotion again. Apparently, Judy had traveled with her to her friend's home.

It wasn't until February 2010 that Judy showed her true valor to Allison. It was late at night, and Allison awoke to a terrible commotion. The dogs were barking, and there was a banging downstairs. Allison attempted to get out of bed but was unable to move. She felt as if she was pinned to the bed. She struggled and fought as the ruckus downstairs escalated, and she began to panic. She was worried about her dogs, and she knew something terrible was happening downstairs, but she was powerless and couldn't move from her bed.

Finally, Allison was released, and she ran downstairs to find the door hanging open and several things knocked over. Apparently, someone had tried to break into her house. Whoever it was had been scared away by something and left the same way they had come. If Allison has been able to get out of bed and investigate, she would have met the burglar head on. The ghost had kept her safe.

There was another incident when Judy was able to help Allison. Allison is very close to her dogs. They are her babies and her best friends. One night, Allison had a party. People were coming and going all night, and in the commotion she lost track of her dogs. She didn't realize that the dogs were gone until the last of her guests had left. Allison panicked. She wanted to go and search the neighborhood for her lost friends. Allison again tried to get up so she could go search for her dogs, but she was held down. Allison fought the ghost again, but by the time she could get up, a neighbor was walking by the window with her two little schnauzers. If Allison had gotten up to search for her dogs, she never would have seen her neighbor walk by with them. She wouldn't have found them.

When Allison talks about her ghost, she calls her "her little visitor." She speaks of the ghost as if she were her friend and her roommate. There is no fear in her voice. Judy is kind and helpful. Her spirit is as friendly as it was in life, and Allison is grateful for all the help Judy has given her over the years. It just goes to show that not all ghosts are scary, and not all hauntings are horrifying. Sometimes even a ghost can become a friend.

THE APPARITIONS OF ATHENS STATE UNIVERSITY

A thens State University is a small school. It isn't well known, even in
Alabama. It is hidden in the far north of the state in the small town
of Athens. It is overshadowed by the many larger, more prestigious schools
in Alabama. The campus, like the university, is small and understated. It is
lined with old oaks that tower over the buildings around them, and you can
almost drive right past the little university. Once you find the campus, you will
be pleasantly surprised by its picturesque serenity. It is beautiful. It looks like
something that fell out of a novel about the Old South. It is quiet, lost in its own
history. There aren't students everywhere, and you might almost imagine the
school to be empty. This might be because many students of this school now
take online classes. Despite the understated nature of the beautiful old school,
Athens State holds a significant place in Alabama history. It is an exercise in
irony, as it is at once the oldest and the youngest university in the state.

Founded in 1822 as the Athens Women's University, Athens State
University was the first postsecondary institution in the state. The entire
community worked together to build this university. Residents wanted a
place where their girls would be raised to be proper southern belles. Since
that time, the university has been renamed and changed administrations
numerous times. Over the years, it has been called Athens Female Institute,
Athens Female College and Athens College. Its last renaming was in 1975,

Athens State University.

when it became Athens State University and also the youngest university in the state. Despite this, the buildings are the same buildings that were there when the school was founded as Athens Women's University in 1822. Whatever their name, these buildings are steeped in the long history of the South. They have seen the plantation age of the South die with the Civil War and watched as North Alabama was reborn.

The Athens campus is much larger now and sprawls out across town. The campus is quiet. The old buildings surround a modern square, where a brick clock tower serves as watchman for the campus. Athens State now serves both male and female students. It is a two-year university that serves those who want to complete a four-year degree after they've already completed a two-year degree. Although it has over twelve hundred teachers, many of them teach online, and the university is very proud of its distance-learning program. Maybe that is why the campus is so quiet. It is a haunting campus, and the most prominent sound when you wander the grounds is the wind rustling through the branches of the trees.

The campus has grown, but the older buildings—Founders Hall, McCandless Hall and Brown Hall—all belong to the greater part of Alabama history. When you step into these old buildings, the floors groan and complain. You can see the age of the buildings in the telltale sagging of the structures. They have born witness to Alabama's sprawling history and have carried its ghosts in their drooping walls.

Founders Hall is the most prominent and oldest building on campus. It was constructed in 1822, and consistent with the religious theme of the building, the four columns in front of the building were named Matthew, Mark, Luke and John. According to tradition, this beautiful building barely survived the Civil War; Union troops planned to burn the building to the ground. The headmistress, Madame Jane Hamilton Childs, was infamous for her strong will and ingenuity. She was a woman to be reckoned with. She was industrious and proactive. When the Union troops arrived, Ms. Childs presented them with a beautifully forged letter from Abraham Lincoln. The letter instructed the troops to leave Founders Hall in peace. After the

Founders Hall.

commanding officer read the letter, he did just that. He never learned that Ms. Child's had never communicated with Abraham Lincoln in any way. Thus, the old building survived the Civil War, and Ms. Childs earned a place in history as one of the cleverest women of the South.

Founders Hall is the most haunted building on campus. It is also the most striking to look at. It is the center of campus, and its dark windows look out on the small parking lot in front it. It is quiet inside the building. Although there are classes upstairs and the administration offices are on one side of the building, visitors can sneak through the quiet halls almost unnoticed. It's easy to imagine that ghosts walk through the halls undetected as well.

There are several ghost stories associated with Founders Hall. The first story comes from the early years of Founders Hall. At that time, the girls lived on the third floor and studied on the lower floors. Founders Hall was the university. One night, a couple of girls attempted to sneak out to meet with their gentleman callers. They lit a candle and snuck into the darkened hall by its wavering light. A sudden gust of wind blew the flame back toward the girls. One of the girls' lovely tresses caught fire, and the girl burst into flames. She died a fiery death on the third floor of Founders Hall beside the long staircase. Her ghost still wanders this hall today. She has been seen in the hall dressed in white carrying a candle. Her footsteps have been heard wandering the corridors, and her face has been seen gazing out of the third-story window. She looks out longingly as if she is still waiting for her gentleman caller, the one she never met.

Another story about Founders Hall describes Ms. Child's stableboy. He was a very nice young man, but he was a bit simple and prone to mischief. Many of the girls fancied him because he was handsome and sweet. They enjoyed his mischievous nature and his practical jokes. He made the girls laugh. The stableboy's name was Bart. Sadly, the poor boy was destined for tragedy. He was kicked in the head by one of the horses and was killed. Shortly after Bart died, strange occurrences began to happen at Founders Hall. Items would go missing and turn up in strange locations. Curtains would move on their own, and cold drafts would pass through warm rooms. Objects were rearranged and misplaced as if someone was continuing Bart's practical jokes. Even in death, Bart seems to have found a way to carry on his mischief. Many have claimed to have seen Bart wandering through Founders Hall. His ghost still lingers there today, and the stories of his

McCandless Hall.

jokes and nonsense carry on, cementing themselves into the long history of Founders Hall.

McCandless Hall is younger than Founders Hall but still rich in history. It is directly next to Founders Hall and sits in the shadow of a large, lazy oak. The building is a Greek Revival–style auditorium. Today, the building houses the Theater Department and has been used for many contemporary plays and musicals. In the early 1900s, it was used to showcase the talent of the famous opera singer Abigail Burns. The story of her stay in Athens is the stuff historical romances are made of. While Ms. Burns's was staying in Athens, she met a local attorney, and the two fell in love almost at first sight. In between performances, the two lovers would meet in the shadows of McCandless Hall. Their love blossomed, and on the night of her final performance, Ms. Burns sung Verdi's opera *La Traviata* with such emotion that those watching wept for the beauty of it.

That night, Ms. Burns had to leave. Her art called her elsewhere, and she could not linger any longer in Athens. She met her lover one last time and made him a solemn promise. "I will return," she vowed. She kissed him and vanished into the night. That night, a terrible storm came to North Alabama, as they often do. Ms. Burns's carriage was capsized, and the lovely Abigail Burns met her death in the mud and rain.

Ms. Burns kept her promise, however. Her ghost returned to McCandless Hall and went to the room where she and her lover had met and exchanged vows. According to legend, she still waits in the shadows. She looks down from the window, waiting for her lover to return to her. Many have seen her face looking out, filled with longing and desire. Others have heard her footsteps and weeping in the dark. When Ms. Burns died, a beech tree was planted in her honor in front of McCandless Hall. The tree still stands there today.

It is possible that Ms. Burns's story is only legend. Research shows no record of her presence at McCandless Hall, and there is no firm evidence to support any of this romantic story. However, those who have seen her ghost and heard her weeping say there is no need for paper documentation. They know what they have seen, and they know that her ghost still roams the halls of McCandless Hall.

Brown Hall is the newest of the haunted buildings on Athens State's campus. It is the least remarkable building of the three, but it has the most remarkable story. The story is remarkable because it tells of heroism and courage in the face of terrible circumstances.

Brown Hall was named in 1912 after Ms. Florence Brown, a teacher and secretary for several years in the early twentieth century. In 1909, a terrible typhoid epidemic swept through Athens. Many fled Athens, fearing contagion. The entire faculty and staff of Athens State fled. Ms. Brown alone remained behind to care for the sick and dying of the university. She nursed them faithfully and ultimately gave her own life for them. Ms. Brown was one of fifteen claimed by typhoid fever in Athens. Brown Hall was dedicated to her in honor of her heroism and self-sacrifice in the face of such a terrible disease. When others fled, she stayed. When others were afraid, she had courage. Her bravery lives on in the legacy of Brown Hall.

There are many who say that she remains in the building that was named for her. She wanders its halls with the others she could not save. Strange lights and odd noises have been seen and heard throughout Brown Hall. Strange footsteps and knocks are not uncommon, but there have been reports of more impressive phenomena. A former continuing-education professor reported levitating objects and knocking sounds cascading, domino-style, around his office until a circuit of the room was completed, at which time things went back to normal. Even though Brown Hall may not be the oldest or most impressive building on this old campus, it certainly has the most impressive story and the most striking haunting.

THE ALBERTVILLE PUBLIC LIBRARY

The Albertville Public Library is one of the most famous haunted libraries in the United States. The online *Encyclopedia Britannica* lists it among one hundred other famous haunted libraries. Mr. George Eberhart of the online encyclopedia describes the library as filled with early morning ghosts. He says the water runs on its own and turns on and off without provocation, and the library is filled with banging and paranormal activity.

By just looking at it, you wouldn't guess that this little library is haunted. Albertville Public Library is a picturesque place. It is a pretty brick building with white trim and flowers in the front. It is famous for its summer reading programs and children's activities. It hosts numerous community events and fun seasonal activities for the family. Chet the Easter Bunny comes for Easter. There are candy egg giveaways for the children. It has a Super Bowl party and regular story times for the children. The Albertville Library seems like the opposite of everything a haunted location should be. The building is new and full of life. It is difficult to imagine any morbid curiosities in this library's history.

Yet the library's history and its haunted history are not completely intertwined. The Albertville Public Library began in a tiny room in the Masonic Lodge. It opened its doors in 1939 with just a little community support. The library floundered, and with the pressures of World War II bearing down upon it, it was forced to close its doors.

The library was started again in 1957, and space in city hall was donated. This time, the library did better. It grew and thrived. In fact, it outgrew its space and had to be moved to a new address on Jackson Street. A new library had to be built. The new library was constructed on an empty lot on Jackson Street, but the lot hadn't always been empty. In fact, the lot had once contained a house that was torn down in the early 1900s. Construction began, and by 1964, the new library was open for business.

The little library did very well on Jackson Street, acquiring rare and antique books. By 1994, the library had over eighty thousand books. About this time, the library received a large donation from the estate of Bob Finney, and a children's section was added on the second floor. The children's section on the second floor offers over three thousand square feet for the children to enjoy and develop a love of reading. The library has continued to grow since then and has even added an elevator.

At first, the ghosts of the library would come in the morning and turn faucets on and off. Water would spill out, and the staff would be frightened, but after the elevator was added, the ghosts were given a new avenue for action. Now, staff members have reported that the elevator goes up and down on its own, along with other ghostly activities. They say that there is loud rapping on the doors, especially in the bathroom and elevator. They also say that this paranormal activity comes mostly in the morning, when the library is first opening up. According to legend, the ghosts of this library are the ghosts of the family who lived in the house that had been demolished in the early 1900s. These ghosts are unhappy that a new building has been placed on top of their home, and they make their anger known by haunting those who visit this little library.

Sadly, the Albertville Public Library has been a victim of disaster recently. The tornados that scoured the earth and made the president declare Albertville a disaster area in the spring of 2010 did significant damage to this piece of the Albertville community. Over $7 million of damage was done in the Albertville area. Ironically, the tornado happened 102 years to the day after the Great Cyclone of 1908, which left an estimated half of the city of Albertville in ruins. In all, twenty-seven people were injured along the storm's path. Although tragedy has struck the library, it is being rebuilt, and the ghosts will soon have a home again.

THE GHOSTS OF RUSSELL CAVERNS

A labama is old. Many people don't realize how old Alabama is. They measure time by the progress of European activity. They don't stop to think of the innumerable natives who once called the state home and left their fingerprints on the history of the state long before the first white people even dreamt of traveling across the ocean. Russell Cave bears witness to this history. For ten thousand years, Russell Cave has been a home to the residents of North Alabama. It has provided them with shelter and water. It gave them a place of refuge in a harsh world. Some say the cave still shelters the ghosts of those who once lived there.

Russell Caverns' story begins in the rock itself. The cave's story began 300 million years ago, when much of Alabama was still underneath an ancient sea. A layer of skeletons and shells from this sea was transformed into limestone by the pressure of water. The world changed, and the area around the cave became dry land. The water that flowed over the land carved holes in the limestone and formed underground streams. The streams cut deeper into the rock. They enlarged the holes, and the holes grew, becoming a cave. The cave was uninhabitable, however, because a large stream flowed through its only opening. Between nine and twelve thousand years ago, a portion of the cave collapsed, making a sinkhole that allowed for further erosion and growth of the cavern structure. This led to the cave's mouth

Russell Caverns.

further expanding in size. The mouth of the cave grew and opened up above the river on the hillside. This portion of the cave became a living area for the paleo and archaic tribes of North Alabama.

The first Native Americans to live in the cave were on the cusp of the paleo and archaic period and were among some of the oldest natives to live in Alabama. A trip to Russell Caverns makes it easy to understand why the cave was inhabited so early in American history. The cave mouth faces east, sheltering it from the harsh north wind. There was a clean water source flowing through the cave. The temperature in the cave would have been warmer in the winter and cooler in the summer. The area was and continues to be filled with wildlife and food.

Russell Caverns was first excavated in 1953. The cave was named after Colonel Thomas Russell. Russell was a veteran of the Revolutionary War, and he owned the land when the first maps of the area were made. After the discovery of the cave and its rich history, the National Geographic Society purchased the land and worked with the Smithsonian Institute to excavate the rich archaeological treasures that lay within the cave. The first artifacts were discovered by the Tennessee Archaeological Society. Shortly after, the excavations were turned over to the Smithsonian, which excavated the cave from 1956 to 1958. The National Geographic Society partially funded the dig. Two tons of artifacts were removed from the site, including pottery, the remains of natives and bone tools. After the excavation, the National Geographic Society donated the land to the American people. The area was made a National Monument by John F. Kennedy in 1961.

What was learned from the cave gave a picture of the lifestyle of the earliest inhabitants of the Americas. The evidence found within Russell Caverns shows one of the longest and most complete archaeological records in the eastern United States. The artifacts found in the cave show human habitation for ten thousand years. The last people to live in the caves lived there around one thousand years ago.

Recent archaeological studies and carbon dating of objects in the cave have shown that the first inhabitants of the cave were Paleo-Indians, and they used the most rudimentary tools and objects for their survival. The Archaic Period showed the most significant use of the cave. The exact habits of those who lived in the cave during this shadowy time in human history seem to be under dispute. Some argue that the cave may have offered a year-round shelter to its occupants, while others say that it is far more likely that the natives used the cave for seasonal periods. Whatever the case, weapons found in the cave include spears, throwing sticks and knives. Bones were used to make needles for sewing and basket weaving. Bone fish hooks have also been found from this period.

After the end of the Woodland Period in 500 CE, Russell Caverns saw less and less use. It is very obvious that those who did visit the caves during the Mississippian Period were just passing through. They left only a few objects behind to show that they had stayed there and had larger, more agricultural villages in other areas. All inhabitation of the cave seems to have ended about one thousand years ago.

Although the Cherokee tribe never used Russell Caverns, today the Cherokee Indians use it for their annual festival. They give demonstrations of native dance, song and craftsmanship. They keep the spirit of the cave alive.

I talked to several people who encountered the ghosts of Russell Caverns, but none wanted his name mentioned. They were hesitant to discuss encounters that they didn't want to accept. One visitor to the cave felt the ghostly presence that is so often experienced there. He was also able to capture a picture with what he described as a ghost in the photograph. Another visitor described phantom noises and a feeling of being ill at ease.

I traveled to the cave on a beautiful spring day. In order to reach Russell Caverns, you have to take a short hike from the visitors' center to the mouth of the cave. Although there are park rangers in the museum, there are no guides in the cave. The rangers are very helpful and friendly. They will talk to you about the history and show you the artifacts that are displayed in the museum. When you walk to the cave, however, you are alone.

The forest is beautiful, and the hike is pleasant. Birds sing above you as you walk. There are hiking trails that continue on above the cave into the verdant forests beyond the more commonly traveled trail. The short trail to the cave is elevated and handicap accessible. The cave is unexpected. It sneaks up on you. A lovely stream flows beneath the elevated walkway and

Inside the cave.

into the enormous mouth of the cave. Slightly above that portion of the cave is an almost separate mouth. This is where the natives lived. It is uncannily quiet here, and those who have seen ghosts have seen them here. They have described seeing faces and spectral bodies amongst the models of natives living their daily lives.

I took a series of pictures at the cave. They were all in the same lighting with the same lens. The first set was perfect, and the second set was filled with a strange fog that drifted through every shot. It seemed to move while I took the picture. I took a deep breath after I saw what had appeared in my photos. My skin crawled, and I walked back to the museum convinced that the many stories told by visitors were true. The ghosts of the natives still live in their old home. They still find shelter in their quiet cave.

THE HOUSE IN THE SHADOW OF MADNESS

McCormick House looks like everything a haunted house should be. It is old and it is large. It's a Queen Anne Revival–style house complete with turrets and spires. The roofline is slightly irregular, and the vibrant colors and alternating textures of the mansion make it unique even among houses of similar size. Some of the outer walls are covered in small stones, and others are bright red. There are bas-reliefs on the outside of the house, and there is a beautiful porch.

The house has forty rooms and is seventeen thousand square feet. There is a basement with its own kitchen, breakfast room, pantry and boiler room. The floors on the first floor are finished with ebony and gold. The ceilings are hand painted, and there is stained glass. The house is in some small degree of disrepair now, and it sits off the road almost staring at those who drive by, daring them to slow down or to stop and look at its gaudy splendor.

Those who do slow down or stop to look at this marvel of an old house will regret it. As soon as a passerby presses the breaks, a woman runs outside and yells. The current residents of McCormick House do not care for visitors. The house is labeled with large no trespassing signs, and it is made very clear that those who are interested in the house's history should stay away. There will be no peace for those who want to know the ghosts of this haunted house. The house has a keeper who regards the secrets of this old mansion as sacred, and she will not abide those who try to look deeper into the shadowy realm within her ghostly abode.

McCormick House was built in 1882 by Major Michael O'Shaughnessy. The major moved from his home in Nashville with his wife, Anna, and their five children. He paid a small fortune for his mansion and filled it with extravagant décor. The décor was legendary, and local papers printed stories about the finery within the house. No expense was spared.

Despite all the work and money put into making McCormick House wonderment, the house was doomed from the beginning. A shadow hung over it. Not long after the major and his family moved into the house, the major went blind. Anne had to sell the house, as they were no longer able to keep up with the sprawling mansion. The house was sold to Mary Virginia McCormick.

Mary McCormick was a wealthy heiress and part of a well-known Chicago family. Her father was Cyrus McCormick, who had invented the reaper. Her brother's wife, Katherine McCormick, would go on to be the major financier and visionary behind the creation of the birth control pill. Despite the enormous fortune and wealth passed on to her by her father, Ms. McCormick also seemed to be cursed. Ms. McCormick was severely mentally ill and suffered spells of such intense madness that she required an entire staff to care for her. According to government archives, both Ms. McCormick and her brother, Stanley, suffered from what was then called dementia praecox. Stanley's mental illness was more famous than Mary's, as it led to several famous court cases and disputes over the then-experimental psychoanalytical treatment techniques. Mary's illness was just as severe as her brother's, however. Today, her condition would be called schizophrenia. Sometimes her illness was so severe that she had to be confined to the basement to prevent her from hurting herself or others. When she wasn't suffering from her bouts of mental illness, Ms. McCormick was an incredibly kind and generous woman. She was known for her philanthropy and generosity and donated large sums of money to many local institutions. Unfortunately, her mental illness eventually crippled her, and she had to be permanently placed in a sanitarium. She had to leave the home she so passionately loved. McCormick House had been her refuge in the storm, and it was very hard for her to let it go.

The house was sold again and fell into despair. It was passed from owner to owner, and none could keep the house or care for it. The paint chipped, and the house's beauty withered. The great estate the house sat on was sold off bit by bit, and rumors of ghosts and hauntings began to circle the house. Many said that Mary McCormick had never left the house and that her ghost still lingered in the basement, bound to it by her madness. From 1932 to 1975, the mansion fell into complete disrepair. The house was in such bad condition that looters began to enter and take pieces of it away. By 1975, the house was an empty shell.

In 1975, the house was purchased by the Reeves, who restored it to its former glory. For a brief period, the house again became known for its beauty. Unfortunately, it was sold in 2004, and the current owners do not like visitors. The house has been closed off, and those who linger too long to look at it are driven away. During the time the house was on the market in 2004, many visitors were able to explore the old structure. Pictures from this period pepper the Internet. Stories of Mary McCormick's ghost also grew during this period. The stories were told by those who walked through the house. They described hearing Mary crying, even during daylight showings of the house. The basement is thought to be particularly haunted, and those who walked through it described a chill and quiet moaning.

Little is known of what has happened since the house sold. Mary's ghost could be quiet now. There is no way to know. Some who have driven by the house and have seen strange shadows lingering in its windows hypothesize that the madness remains in the house with Mary's ghost. There are over two thousand posts on Citydata.com about the McCormick House. I have not posted the details of the city where this house is located or any pictures here to protect the current residents. However, the city data on the area is filled with descriptions of the house and what visitors have witnessed in and around the house. They serve as evidence to the continued fascination with this haunted location. The stories about this house may have faded with time and secrecy, but they haven't died. The conclusion about this house by visitors is always the same: McCormick House still lives in the shadow of madness, and Mary's ghost lingers within, reaching out to all those who will listen.

THE TUTWILER HOTEL

The Tutwiler Hotel is gone. Its graceful form no longer adds to the beauty of the Birmingham skyline. Its shadows no longer darken the streets, and all those who have stayed there have been lost in history. The Tutwiler was imploded in 1992 to make room for a bank, and like many things in Birmingham, Alabama, it was lost to the pages of history.

Birmingham, Alabama, is a city built from fire. In the early parts of the twentieth century, it defined itself as one of the largest producers of steel in the country. The areas around Birmingham had significant deposits of iron, coal and limestone. These were all the ingredients for steel, and their presence set the stage for the emergence of Birmingham as a massive steel producer. If you explore Birmingham, you'll see the evidence of the importance of steel in the landscape. Sloss Furnace is an important city center and is used for concerts, performances and festivals. It is an abandoned steel mill. There is a large statue of Vulcan on a mountain above the city. He is the god of the city and its protector. He was the god of blacksmithing and fire.

Like Birmingham, the Tutwiler was also built from fire. Robert Jemison built the hotel as a lodging place for all the steel industry professionals who traveled to the city. He built it for the most important people in the industry, the members of the American Steel Institute, so they could meet in Birmingham in luxury and style. The hotel was also financed by the steel

The Tutwiler Hotel.

industry; Jemison's backers were all important players in the steel industry. One of the first people to back the construction of the Tutwiler was George Crawford, president of the Tennessee Coal, Iron and Railroad Company. Additional backing came from Major Tutwiler, who was president of the Coal and Coke Company in Birmingham.

Together, these men recruited the best builders and architects from around the country to build a hotel of such luxury and beauty that it would put all others to shame. Building began on this magnificent hotel in 1913 and was completed in 1914. The hotel was everything it was promised to be. It had an elegant main lobby filled with chandeliers. Large balconies overlooked the lobby from two mezzanine levels. The hotel had 343 luxurious rooms, and each one was decorated with care. The building also had many meeting rooms, including eight large rooms that opened to make a grand ballroom that could accommodate twelve hundred people.

Birmingham and its steel industry continued to grow and prosper, and the Tutwiler prospered with the city. However, like many industrial cities,

Birmingham saw a decrease in growth in the later part of the century. Many of the old steel companies began to die, and as the steel industry began to die, so did the Tutwiler. The Tutwiler fell into disrepair as steel faded from prominence in Vulcan's city. In 1971, the hotel was imploded to make room for progress.

The city didn't forget the Tutwiler, however, and when Birmingham's economy began to thrive and prosper again, investors began to think about reinventing the Tutwiler. Again, Birmingham found itself needing a luxurious downtown hotel. According to an article in the *Birmingham News*, "There is a market for a small, independently owned hotel that would appeal to executives."

At the time this need was discovered, the Ridgeley Apartment Building in downtown Birmingham was a lovely old building occupied mostly by senior citizens. It was a hotel/apartment building, and although it had a few permanent residents, many of those living in it were only staying there for a brief period of time. The building was striking, and hotel management thought that it would be perfect for the new Tutwiler Hotel.

The Ridgeley Apartments were built by Major Tutwiler in 1914, the same year that construction began on the original Tutwiler. Many of the people who lived in these apartments had lived there for their entire lives. Although the building wasn't important to many people, those who called it home loved it greatly. Most of its residents had no intention of ever leaving. When the news came to the residents that the Ridgeley Apartments were being bought out by a hotel company, they were devastated. One employee of the Ridgeley said that when the night officers of the Tutwiler Investment Co., which owned the building, came in and told the residents that they would have to be out of the building within the month, it led to great sorrow. This was hard news for the occupants of Ridgeley Apartments. Although the building was mostly empty, for those who remained in the apartment/hotel, it was the only home they had ever known. One employee commented on the tenants' reactions to the news by saying, "It was very discouraging for many of the tenants because they lived there so long."

But nothing stops progress, and by 1985, renovations of the Ridgeley had commenced. All of the old occupants of the building had been evicted. The architectural firm of Kidd/Plosser/Sprague was hired to renovate and restore the run-down Ridgeley and turn it into the Tutwiler Hotel.

Birmingham City received a huge grant for the Ridgeley Project, and it cost almost $15 million to restore the old building. The Ridgeley was reinvented and renamed. It was given the name of a hotel that had once been famous but had been forgotten and demolished. The Tutwiler opened its doors again on December 13, 1986. There was an enormous gala dinner to celebrate the occasion, and funds raised by the gala were donated to the Birmingham Historical Society.

The Tutwiler Hotel is beautiful. It is eight stories and has some of its predecessor's glory. The 149-room hotel has 53 suites, 96 regular rooms, 4 banquet and meeting rooms and a restraint and bar. The lobby is a little work of art. It has marble floors and chandeliers. It has two rooms off to the side that have been decorated with period décor to establish a sense of history within the building. One of the first-floor meeting rooms has dark-stained oak beams and terra-cotta cornices. These rooms are popular locations for weddings and conferences. The guest rooms are comfortable and clean, and the food at the restaurant is good. Perhaps because of this, some of the previous occupants of the Ridgeley don't want to leave their once-beloved home. The Tutwiler Hotel is famous for its ghosts and is listed among the most haunted hotels in the nation.

I traveled to Birmingham to find the most famous ghost in the Tutwiler. This ghost has often been called Major Tutwiler, and most of the employees of the hotel know him by name. Most don't think he is actually the ghost of Major Tutwiler, but the name has stuck. It is possible that the ghost *is* the major, however. He did live in the Ridgeley Apartments. But the ghost has left no evidence of his identity in his behavior or otherwise.

The story of the major begins when the Tutwiler first reopened. Every night, the bartender would close down the restaurant and turn off all the lights in the kitchen and bar area. Every morning, he would find them on again. This went on for some time, and eventually the bartender's manager complained about him leaving the lights on every night. The bartender wanted to defend his job, so he invited his manager to join him in his nightly rounds. The manager joined him the next evening, and they turned off all the lights together.

The next morning, the lights were on again, and the good major added to his activity by taking out dishes and food, turning on the ovens and leaving a mess in the kitchen. The next evening, the bartender tried something new. He closed everything down and called out into the empty restaurant, "Good Night. Please clean up after yourself and turn all the lights off when you are done!"

The next day, everything was in order. So a tradition was begun in which, each night, whoever closes down the restaurant and bar says goodnight to Major Tutwiler. I asked several employees about the ghosts of the Tutwiler. Many knew about the story of Major Tutwiler, and each employee told me a slightly different version of the same story. I wasn't surprised by any of this because the story of Major Tutwiler is fairly well known.

I *was* surprised by a different story that I was told by two other employees. These employees worked in the hotel and not the restaurant. According to them, there is another ghost in the Tutwiler. This ghost came from the Ridgeley.

They described a little girl who wanders the halls on the sixth floor. This little girl is partial to rooms 603 and 604, and in life, she had lived in the apartment that occupied these rooms. The little girl fell ill and died in those rooms. Her ghost has never left the Ridgeley, and she still wanders the halls looking for playmates and making herself known to those who stay in rooms 603 or 604. The staff members of the hotel describe hearing her footsteps in the hall and her laughter. They also tell the story of one staff member who actually saw the little girl's ghost in room 603. This staff member was cleaning the room, and when she turned around, she saw a small girl standing behind her. The child was diaphanous and faded away as quickly as she had appeared, but she had been visible long enough to be identified as a young child.

The little girl's ghost used to be called "the knocker" because she would knock on guests' doors and then vanish. She often showed a preference for female guests. There are many stories in the Tutwiler about terrified guests calling the front desk in the middle of the night to complain about the banging on their door. Room 604 appears to be her favorite haunt. She's kept guests in this room up all night. This knocking behavior reminds me of a game we used to play when I was a little girl and we were feeling mischievous. We would run up and down the neighborhood ringing doorbells and running away. We called this "ding-dong ditching." Maybe this little girl is keeping up with her childish pranks.

I stayed at the Tutwiler on a chilly winter night. My two sons were with me, and they were excited to see if there were any real ghosts at the Tutwiler.

The sixth floor of the Tutwiler Hotel.

Our room was beautiful, and the staff was pleasant. The history in the hotel was everywhere, and every room was marked with a different historical landmark in the Birmingham area. It was clear that the Tutwiler was proud of its history and its place in Birmingham's past.

While we were at the Tutwiler, we stayed in room 602, adjacent to and sharing a balcony with room 603. Although we slept soundly and were not bothered by any paranormal activity or knocking, my son woke up early and took pictures of the little balcony outside our window. All of his pictures were crowded with the strangest mist, and he reports hearing a little girl whisper.

A FRENCH WIFE'S TALE

Huntsville, Alabama, has become a city of immigrants. The immigrants come from all over the country and all over the world. In a little over fifty years, Huntsville has grown from a small town of a little over 13,000 to a thriving metropolis of over 200,000. This has led to the birth of a city that is populated mostly by non-natives. The residents of Huntsville are, for the most part, not southerners. Even if they were born in Huntsville, their parents came from different states and different countries. Huntsville is a city that pays homage to a German immigrant for defining it as the "Rocket City," and its population reflects this.

One of the many non-natives to immigrate to Huntsville, Alabama, in the 1970s was a French woman named Nicole. Nicole had just been married and was pregnant with her first child when she moved to Alabama. She had come to the United States with her husband. Her husband was a scholar from Yale who had taken a job at the University of Alabama in Huntsville. Nicole immediately disliked Alabama. It wasn't that she only loved France, because she had lived in many other countries and places, but she just couldn't make herself happy in Alabama.

Nicole's story began long before she moved to Alabama. She was born in France, and her mother wept when she was born. She cried because she had wanted sons, and the little girl was an unwelcome addition to the family. This moment defined Nicole's life. Her mother told her the story many times, and whether or not it was true, it was critical to the way Nicole would grow up and perceive the world.

When Nicole was still young, her family moved from France. Her father was in the military, and he had been transferred to Vietnam. At the time, Vietnam was still a French colony, and French soldiers had to be stationed there. Nicole grew up in Vietnam, raising her younger brothers and sister. She learned to cook and fell in love with the foreign landscape. When her family moved again, they moved to another French colony. This time, they were stationed in Algeria. Nicole moved with her family and transitioned as well as anyone. She had become the primary caretaker for the children, and she had grown to love this role. She cleaned and cooked. She had begun to find art in cooking, which was a passion she would carry with her for her entire life.

When her family moved back to France, Nicole went with them. She set up her life in conjunction with her family's needs. She got a job and helped her brothers with money when they needed it. When her siblings got married and had children, she took care of them during the days. She was always the caregiver. She was expected to give money and take care of the others. She was never expected to have any needs or wants of her own. This is the role that had been forced on her by her mother, and Nicole would carry the emotional burden that came from inheriting this role for the rest of her life.

When she was in her twenties, Nicole tried to break free from her family. She tried to have an adventure of her own and establish her own life. She moved to Morocco and got a job. In Morocco, she was happy for a while, but tragedy brought her back to France. Nicole never named the tragedy. She wouldn't dare speak of it. She only said that she could no longer stay abroad. She went home and resumed her life as caretaker.

Nicole lived this way for many years. Her mother had berated her into believing that it was all she deserved. She spent her life taking care of others' children and began to give up hope of having any of her own. In 1974, her family introduced her to a professor who had been living abroad in America. The professor was older than she was. He was a professor in a place she had never heard of in the United States: the University of Alabama in Huntsville. He had his own life and history. He had been married twice before and had a grown son in France. He also had several adopted children from a previous marriage in the United States. Nicole was quite taken with the professor, and when he returned to the States, the two agreed to write to each other.

A great love blossomed from this correspondence. Nicole was utterly swept away by the power of the professor's language and the beauty of his poetry. She fell in love with his words and found herself dreaming of going away with him to a new world across the ocean. The professor was also quite taken with Nicole. She had never had a formal education, but she was a prolific writer and spent her nights immersed in books about history. She was intelligent and witty, and her tragic past appealed to the professor's need to rescue her.

When the professor returned to France, he asked Nicole to marry him, and she agreed. For the first time in a long time, Nicole was hopeful and her expectations were high. By the time the two were married, she was already pregnant with their first and only son. The journey was nothing new for Nicole. She had traveled before, but Alabama was not the America she expected. Nicole was an artist in the kitchen and found herself crushed by the limited food choices available at the local markets. She had also been accustomed to going to the boulanger and patisserie every day. In France, she would walk. These things were completely unavailable to Nicole in Alabama. Nicole also never learned to drive. Cars made her nervous, and she had never needed a car in France or anyplace else. In Alabama, Nicole was completely isolated without a car. She was in a strange land and didn't know the language as well as she could. She felt lost and depressed. Southern culture was baffling to her, and she knew that she would never fit into this strange land.

To make matters worse, although her husband was brilliant and kind, he was often lost in his books and intellectual pursuits. He spent much of his time at work, leaving her alone. When he was home, he wanted to read and study. He was somewhat absentminded about day-to-day life and would forget things that mattered to her, like birthdays and anniversaries. He didn't understand her sorrow and was at a loss about how to help her adapt. He was not the doting romantic she had expected from his letters. Additionally, his past was disturbing to her. He didn't pay as much attention as she thought he should to his son in France, and his stepchildren in America took all his financial resources without offering any love or appreciation in return. In fact, once they were grown and their braces paid for, they forgot all about him, leaving him deeply in debt. Nicole was desolate. There was no family, and there wasn't enough money. Nicole didn't know what to do. Loneliness and isolation pulled her into a well.

The birth of her son brought a brief reprieve from this well. She found happiness in her new baby and took him back to France every summer. She raised her son in between worlds, and she gave him all the love she could. He was brought up in France with his cousins, and for a brief period every year, Nicole found true joy in watching her son play with her brothers' and sister's children. She finally had a life of her own. These windows of joy were brief, however, and her depression crept up on her. Before the boy was grown, she started losing herself in tearful spells. She found reprieve in her writing and in caring for other people's children, but Alabama was taking its toll on her. Nicole made a few friends, many of whom were either foreign or academics. She grew close to them, but when her son left for school, no amount of friends could save her from her sorrow.

Over the following years, Nicole spent more and more time in France. Yet even France offered little comfort. Her family was torn apart by bickering and fighting, and she was the last of the family to bring them together. She was still trying to take care of everyone and make everything better. That had always been her job, but she quickly learned that her move across the ocean made it impossible for her to hold her family together any longer. Her son got married and quickly had two children. Nicole's heart was lost in her grandchildren, so when her husband died, she still couldn't return home. She remained trapped in a country that she never loved and that had never understood her.

Nicole died unexpectedly. She was cremated and buried with her husband in Hampton Cove. Her grave lies in between two mountains in the shade. Her family saved a portion of her ashes to carry back to France and cast into the sea. This had been her final request. She wanted to be laid to rest in France.

Nicole had been petulant in life. She had high expectations of her friends and loved ones, and no one ever really met her expectations. In death, nothing changed. Her best friend was the first one to tell me about Nicole's ghost. Her best friend was also French, and they had shared many years together and had a lot in common. Her friend went to Nicole's funeral, but several months had passed, and her friend hadn't returned to the grave site to lay flowers on the grave. Her friend began to feel a presence in her home, and she felt that the presence was angry. Things went missing or moved to a different location. Her friend knew that Nicole's ghost was in her house, and Nicole was angry that she hadn't gone back to the grave. A week later, her friend took flowers to the grave and laid them there. The haunting stopped, and her friend hasn't been bothered ever since.

Nicole's family, however, hasn't been released yet. At first, it was the children who knew the ghost was in the house. The boys would come running down the stairs looking for Nicole, and when their mother asked them why they were looking, they would say they had heard their grandma calling. Her youngest grandson claims he saw her sitting in the old chair where she had spent her days and nights. The dogs bark at the old china cabinet that the family inherited from Nicole. The china cabinet is where the last piece of Nicole sits in an ebony urn, waiting to be returned to France. The daughter-in-law has also seen Nicole in her house. She spends a lot of time alone at night after the children go to bed. One night, the dogs started barking at the china cabinet, and the daughter-in-law got up to see what they were barking at. The garage door opened suddenly and the woman was confronted head-on with a ghost standing directly in front of her.

No one in the family feels that Nicole's ghost is hostile; they feel that she is waiting. She is spending her time with the grandchildren she loved so dearly, while she waits to finally go home to the country she missed so deeply.

THE HAUNTING OF
SWEET WATER MANSION

The Sweet Water Plantation was the largest plantation in the southern United States. This enormous plantation occupied thirty-eight hundred acres across northern Alabama and had about 247 slave workers. It was a thing of beauty, and it was the epitome of all the elegance and grace the old plantation South had to offer. Sweet Water Plantation still stands in Florence, Alabama, and can be found off Florence Boulevard. Those who know Sweet Water know that it is the most haunted place in Florence; ghost stories drift out of it like a steady fog. The ghosts that walk its halls are many, and their stories fill the house's history with darkness and sorrow.

Sweet Water Plantation was built by a man named John Brahan. John Brahan was made receiver of public monies for the land office in Nashville in 1809. Through this position, he was able to purchase the vast amounts of land the mansion resides on in the great land sale of 1818.

Brahan was plagued by bad luck, and his primary residence in Huntsville burned to the ground shortly after he purchased this land. He then decided to move to one of the tracks he had purchased in the northwest of the state. He chose this tract of land for its beauty. It had a large spring that emptied into the Tennessee River. It was a beautiful area, and the natives called it *Succatania*—a valley paradise where the water is sweet and clear. Brahan decided to keep this name for his home, calling it Sweet Water Plantation.

Brahan began construction on his home in paradise in 1828. He put his blood, sweat and tears into the vast estate and went so far as to make the clay bricks with his own hands. His house was a vision that would take some time to create. He wanted all the details to be perfect. He spent his final years working in vain to complete his vision. Unfortunately, Brahan's bad luck persisted, and in 1938 he died of pneumonia. His body was buried in the shadow of his incomplete dream. He would never see Sweet Water Plantation in life. He would never see the glorious plantation it would become.

He had willed the house to his son, but his son was a city dweller, and the house was sold to Robert M. Patton. Patton had better luck than Brahan. In 1832, Patton finished Sweet Water. He was also elected to the state legislature. Eventually, Patton would go on to be elected governor in 1865. Patton was able to complete Sweet Water Mansion. He followed Brahan's original plan, and the house was everything Brahan had wanted it to be. The house was stunning, two stories tall and had wallpaper that had been brought from New York. Three sprawling porches surrounded the house. There was a weaving room and an icehouse. It had a full basement and an expansive wine cellar. There were twenty slave cabins that were used to house the numerous slaves.

Patton had nine children, and his family occupied Sweet Water for over 130 years. The house was visited by all the great names of the South. General Andrew Jackson and Confederate president Jefferson Davis both graced the halls of this sprawling mansion. Unfortunately, the house was also visited by sorrow.

Three of Patton's sons left to fight in the Civil War. His oldest son was shot and died in the Battle of Shiloh. The boy's slave brought his body back to the house for burial. Patton invited everyone to the funeral, and the entire community came and showed their support. The house was filled with mourners. Black skirts swished across pine floors, and the sound of weeping echoed through the elaborate plantation house. The boy was buried in the family cemetery with great lamentation.

According to legend, ever since this time, at midnight on rainy nights the sounds of mourning return to Sweet Water Plantation. Over the steady drip of rain, the weeping of women can be heard. The gentle sweeping of phantom skirts can be heard brushing against the hard pine floor. You can hear a piano playing funeral music, and if you go to the front of the house, you can see a funeral process gliding down the darkened staircase in the waning light of night. If you follow the procession, you can see the entire funeral. You can see the young Patton's coffin in the dark and walk through the ghosts of his mourning family.

The Civil War brought much sorrow to the South and to Sweet Water Plantation. The death of a beloved son was almost impossible to bear, but the war would do more damage than that. General Sherman passed through Florence on his dreaded march through the South. He left ghosts behind him at the University of North Alabama, and he also left ghosts at Sweet Water Mansion.

Sherman raided Sweet Water Mansion and took everything of value from the old house. He used the slave cabins to house the sick and dying and burned those who died on the premises. Many ghosts have been seen walking the grounds of Sweet Water. The Yankee ghosts of those dead soldiers who were left behind by Sherman are amongst their legions. Visitors and caretakers alike have described the many soldier ghosts that still wander the grounds of Sweet Water.

So many ghosts have been seen at Sweet Water that they are almost impossible to name. The ghost of Brahan himself is said to linger in the shadows of the old house. He mingles with the funeral guests that wander on rainy nights. A lonely white lady has also been seen in Sweet Water Mansion. She wanders, as if lost, searching for something she left behind.

For many years, Sweet Water was abandoned and left to disrepair. The owners put up No Trespassing signs and prevented the curious from learning the old house's many stories. The building became a ruin that housed only ghosts. Recent development has changed that. Now, the curious can visit Sweet Water. The house has been renovated and brought back to life.

Last Halloween, Sweet Water opened its doors as a haunted attraction. Ghost story enthusiasts came from all over North Alabama to finally view the spectacular haunted mansion in hopes that they might catch a glimpse of some phantom. The reviews of this haunted attraction were numerous; some people loved it and claimed to have caught a glimpse of another world, while others said that it was too slow compared to more fast-paced haunted attractions. Whatever their opinion of the tour, many came just to stand among the many ghosts of Sweet Water.

ABOUT THE AUTHOR

Jessica Penot, a Huntsville resident, is a behavioral health therapist with an MS in clinical psychology. As an award-winning fiction writer, ten of her short stories have been published in a variety or magazines and journals, and she has written a horror novel due out by the end of 2010. She writes a popular blog about ghosts and hauntings, averaging 150 hits a day, and she is a member of the American Ghost Society, the American Ghost Hunter's Society, the Horror Writer's Association and the Penn Writer's Association.

Visit us at
www.historypress.net

CPSIA information can be obtained
at www.ICGtesting.com
Printed in the USA
BVHW091015260819
556809BV00016B/988/P